McDOUGAL'S GLEN

By James E. Graham

Cover Artist: Mark Brayer

Trilogy Christian Publishers
A Wholly Owned Subsidiary of Trinity Broadcasting Network
2442 Michelle Drive
Tustin, CA 92780
Copyright © 2024 by James E. Graham.

All rights reserved, including the right to reproduce this book or portions thereof in any form whatsoever.
For information, address Trilogy Christian Publishing Rights Department, 2442 Michelle Drive, Tustin, CA 92780.
Trilogy Christian Publishing/ TBN and colophon are trademarks of Trinity Broadcasting Network.
For information about special discounts for bulk purchases, please contact Trilogy Christian Publishing.

Trilogy Disclaimer: The views and content expressed in this book are those of the author and may not necessarily reflect the views and doctrine of Trilogy Christian Publishing or the Trinity Broadcasting Network.

10 9 8 7 6 5 4 3 2 1
Library of Congress Cataloging-in-Publication Data is available.
ISBN 979-8-89041-706-0
ISBN 979-8-89041-707-7 (ebook)

Disclaimer

This is a work of fiction. Angus McDougal, his family, the glen, and everything associated with it are fabricated. Various historical figures have been intertwined into the story purely for the story's sake.

There is an actual McDougal clan in Scotland with their own tartan variations. The kilt on the front cover is a facsimile of the ancient tartan.

DEDICATION

This book is dedicated to my mother, Louise Fausett Graham. At an early age, she introduced me to the world of books. My reading skills were abysmal, and something had to be done. She took me to the library. It was the best thing she could have done because I discovered a love for books that is with me to this day.

If not for my mother, I wouldn't have written this story or the others I have put to paper. She has passed on to her reward. But if she were alive, she would encourage me to pursue my passion. She would be my number one fan.

"Thanks, Mom!"

Contents

THE GLEN..9
MOVING IN..17
BUILDING A HOME....................................21
EXPLORING THE GLEN.................................27
INDIANS!...35
CHRISTMAS..41
THE WEDDING..49
THE SUPPLY RUN.....................................59
TRADING POST.......................................67
THE STALLION.......................................77
BREAKING THE BLACK.................................85
TRAGEDY ON THE RIVER...............................91
THE TURKEY SHOOT..................................107
THE HERD..113
THE RUNAWAY.......................................127
OBADIAH SKINKS....................................137
CROWS!..143
RUSTLERS..153
SKELETON CANYON...................................165

GOING FOR SUPPLIES	173
FAMILY	185
LITTLE ANGUS & SALLY MAY	189
THE POKER GAME	199
THE BLIZZARD	211
GOING SWIMMING	219
A LIFE SHARED	225
SPOOKED!	235
LITTLE PEOPLE	245
BEAR PROBLEMS	249
JOSEPH	257
RONDYVOO	263
THE DREAM	271
BLESSED	275
THE BIRTHDAY	279
THE GLEN OF BLESSINGS	283
THE STROKE	289
IT HAPPENED IN CHURCH	295
KATHERINE	301
A CHISELED ROCK	305

THE GLEN

"Boys, we're here!" shouted Angus while reining in his horse. "I can remember it like it was yesterday. See that big pile of rocks across the river? That's my claim marker. It took me most of a day to gather all those rocks. I knew I could find my way back. Praise the Lord Almighty that I did!"

They were at the Snake River in Idaho. It was the McDougal family. The patriarch, Angus, had discovered the valley while he was with a trapping party in 1823. He was smitten with the beauty of the valley the first time he saw it and immediately claimed it. He had erected a stone marker. Then, he chiseled his name and date to signify the valley was his.

Now, it was twenty-six years later. They were here to take possession. They had left St. Louis with a large wagon train bound for Oregon, crossed into Idaho, and parted company with the wagon train when they reached the Snake River. Angus had led the family upriver until he found what he was looking for. For many years, he had told his family about the valley. Now they were here, eighty-eight in total, his sons, daughters, their families, and hired hands. He and his wife, Katherine, had been blessed with eleven children. All had survived childhood and were virile and healthy. There were seven boys and four girls—Ansel, Atticus, Anne, Absalom, Abigail, Abraham, Abner, Amelia, Alexander, Ava, and Little Angus. All but Amelia, Alexander, and Little Angus were married and had their own families.

Everyone had either dismounted or crawled down from a wagon seat and gathered at the river's edge.

"Pa, are you sure this is the place?" asked Abraham.

"I know this country like the back of my hand. Do you see that boulder up there? I carved my name, date, and claim on that stone. I'm sure of it," answered Angus.

"Pa, how are we going to get across?" asked Ansel while staring at the river. "The water looks pretty rough, and where is the valley? All I see is a granite cliff ahead of us."

"It's too late in the day to try crossing the river. We'll camp on this side tonight and get a fresh start in the morning. Everybody needs a hot meal and a good night's sleep. Besides that, the women are exhausted. Tomorrow is going to be a chore," he answered.

No one got any sleep that night. Everyone was too excited and anxious. The place they had dreamed of for so many years was across the river. Their dream was about to become a reality.

At daybreak, the men stood on the riverbank and

pondered how to get across safely.

"We'll try to float the wagons across. We have to be careful. There are plenty of rocks and rapids to worry about," decided Angus. "We'll tie ropes to the corners of the wagons and use the horses to help steer them across. One of us on each corner should do it. The valley is there. Don't you worry about it; we'll do just fine."

Considering there were twenty-eight heavily loaded wagons, it wouldn't be easy. It took most of the day, and they almost lost one of them. The current had caught it and almost jerked it out of their hands. It was starting to topple over when the men regained control.

"Whew! That was close! That wagon has my blacksmith tools and anvil in it," sighed an exhausted Atticus in relief. He had fussed and worried about it ever since they had left home.

Finally, they were safely across. That included their horse remuda, cattle, chickens, and hogs.

After cleaning up, Angus called all of the family together. His trapping friends had called him Preacher because of his faith in God. The name had stuck, and many only knew him by that name. Now he called for silence.

Bowing his head, he began, "Let us pray. Father, we thank you for your traveling mercies. We thank you that we got here safely. We thank you for our new home in the valley. We ask that you bless us, protect us, and meet our needs. In Jesus's almighty powerful name. Amen."

They circled their wagons and unhitched the teams while the women started a fire and began fixing supper.

"Pa, how did you find this place?" Abner asked while they were eating.

"It was pure luck. I was following the river, looking for beaver, when I saw an elk disappear behind that massive rock up there," he said as he pointed at a boulder against the cliff wall. "We needed meat, so I went after it. Behind that rock is a big hole in the cliff. I followed that elk into a large cave. On the other side is the valley. Just wait until you see it."

"Can we go now?" asked Little Angus.

"We'll go in the morning after everyone's had a good night's sleep. I will show you the valley in the morning," he glared at Little Angus.

"Aw, Pa!"

"You heard me!"

It was a restless night for everyone. It had been a long, arduous journey, and they were exhausted, but excitement and anticipation kept them awake.

Morning broke with the sun popping over the horizon. The aroma of bacon and sourdough biscuits caused everyone to linger near the cooking fires. The men stood around with steaming hot cups of coffee to help ward off the morning chill.

After eating, Angus rose to his feet and spoke. "Quiet down, everybody. I know that you are anxious to see your new home. We're going to do it now. We'll divide up into two groups. One has to stay and watch over the camp while the others go. When the first group returns, it will be the other group's turn."

The family groaned with disappointment.

"Who gets to go first, Pa?"

"It is only fair that your ma, the five oldest, and their families go first."

"Aw, Pa, I wanted to go first!" complained Little Angus.

"Hush up, boy, or you won't go!"

Chastised, Little Angus decided he had better keep his mouth shut.

"Boys, get your rifles. We don't know what might be behind those rocks," ordered Angus.

Angus led the first party from the camp. Following a game trail up the hill, they approached the rock. Angus ducked behind it, and they entered a large cavern. It was massive. There were signs of animal activity everywhere. On one of the walls, there were primitive paintings of stick-figure people and animals. At the other end of the cave, they could see the bright glow of sunlight emanating from a large hole.

"I figure we can winter in here while building our cabins," offered Angus. "It's dry, and if my memory serves me right, there's a spring on the other side of that wall."

Some of them nodded their heads in agreement.

Leading them farther, they stepped out of the cave entrance onto a bench overlooking the valley. They couldn't comprehend what they saw. The valley opened in front of them. It was vast and surrounded by steep granite walls as far as the eye could see. In the distance, they could see a large lake fed by a waterfall that cascaded from a fissure in the rock. They watched a herd of elk, smiled and pointed as eagles soared overhead, and were thrilled at seeing a herd of wild horses heading for the lake.

"Oh, Angus! It's bonnie!" gushed Kate. "Much better than you described!" The magnitude of it had taken her breath away.

"Aye! Words don't do it justice," he replied as he watched his children's reactions.

"How big is it?"

"It's hard to tell. I'm figuring somewhere around forty thousand acres, give or take a few."

Stunned at his answer, they stood and stared. Their homestead in Tennessee had been forty acres of hills and ravines. It was more than they could comprehend.

"Pa, while you were trapping, Ma told us that you would look for a new place for us to live. As a boy, I always wondered what it would be like. You have beat all of my expectations to a frazzle," said an amazed Ansel. "When you came home and told us about it, the story sounded too good to be true. I'll never doubt you again."

"Is this the only entrance?"

"I don't know for sure. We'll have to do some exploring," answered Angus.

"We can run a huge herd here. We can have a horse ranch too and do whatever we want," added Atticus.

"Aye, we can," answered Angus as he took Kate into his arms. "I have one more thing to say."

"What is it?"

"Welcome home. Welcome to McDougal's Glen. Let's go back so I can show the valley to the rest of the family. Please, don't spoil it by telling them what you've seen. I want them to see for themselves," said Angus.

That night, Kate and Angus were cuddling in their blankets under their wagon.

"You old coot! Why didn't you tell me it was such a bonnie glen?" asked Kate while elbowing him in the ribs.

"I couldn't have described it to you if I had all the words in the world to use," he answered. "What does it justice? Magnificent,? Grand? Awesome? You tell me what fits it?"

"Kate thought for a moment and answered. "Bonnie!"

"My thoughts exactly."

"Good night, my bonnie Kate," he said as he kissed her.

"Good night, and I love you," she responded.

MOVING IN

Supper that night was a happy affair. Everybody was excited, laughing and joking with each other. Angus let them have their fun. They deserved it. It had been a long trip.

Afterward, he called them all together.

"Quiet down, everybody! We've got some things to talk about," he announced. "I need your attention, please."

Everybody settled down, and he continued.

"You saw the glen today. Now, we have some decisions to make. It's only fair that we make the decisions by voting. There are eleven of you, and I make it twelve. In case of a tie, the deciding vote will be by your mother. Does everybody agree with that?"

Everybody agreed, and Angus went on.

"Something we must consider and be ready for is that we will probably have to fight for our glen. I'm sure the Indians consider it belongs to them and won't want to give it up. There may be someone else who will try to claim it. I know that the Shoshone tribe is prominent in this area. I've had dealings with them in the past. Time will tell as far as ownership. As far as I'm concerned, it's ours until proven wrong."

"Whatever it takes, Pa!"

"We're prepared to fight. We brought enough powder and ball to fight a small war. I know that for a fact. I drove the wagon it was in," offered Little Angus.

"As for me and my family, we're here to stay," offered a defiant Absalom.

"Aye, I feel that way too," replied Angus. "Tomorrow, we need to fence a small corral for the livestock. While the men are fencing, the women can start moving into the cave. I think we can squeeze the wagons inside once we clear the path. It will be a good place to store them for future use. We can fix this cave. It can be downright bonnie for the winter. Even the lads and lasses can help. We need as much firewood as we can get. Send the young ones out for wood now. We'll need it for the breakfast fire. Everybody, let's get busy."

They posted guards and turned in for the night. The guards rotated every four hours so that the men got some sleep that night. Morning came, and everybody was up early, hungrily ate breakfast, and waited for Angus.

"I think we need to get the wagons inside first because if we are out of sight, we are safe. The fencing can wait until afterward. It shouldn't take too long."

It was an understatement. There were boulders they had to move and a path they had to clear. Using teams of horses and ropes, they began inching the boulders out of the way. After many long hours, it was ready to be used. Unloading each wagon came next. They carried the cargo uphill into the cave. Then, the canvas coverings and the hoop supports were carefully removed and stored. The men moved the wagons into the cave. It was back-breaking work, and all of them were tired.

Once inside, they had to push the heavy Conestoga wagons over the uneven floor. After three days of this, the men were exhausted. Moving the last wagon against the cave wall, the men went out on the bench and collapsed. The women brought them cold dippers of water and something to eat.

"Finally," muttered Abner while stretching, "my back is killing me."

"What about my foot?" moaned Atticus. "You backed a wagon over it! Lucky it isn't broke!"

The men laughed at his discomfort. They all had their aches and pains.

"I didn't think it would take us three days to do it. We'll do the fencing the day after tomorrow. We'll hobble the horses tonight. They won't go far. Let's help the women get everything carried into the cave. I know they can't carry the blacksmith anvil and tools," said Angus.

Groaning, the men got to their feet and helped the women.

Each family chose a spot in the cave as their own. The sleeping quarters were situated so that each family would have some privacy. They started a fire to see if the cave's fissures would draw the smoke out. To their surprise, the smoke dissipated and didn't cloud the cave. Katherine chose a good spot for the large cooking fire. Some of the young men made make-shift tables for their meals. Rocking chairs appeared around the fire, and the men made torches to light the area.

In a far corner, Angus built chicken coops. The milk cows and hogs had a pen constructed as well. It was bedtime before they had it done. Everybody had gone to bed except for the guards. Angus and Kate were sitting by the fire. He wrapped his arms around Kate and spoke.

"Well, what do you think?"

"I think for a pair of old Scots, we've done pretty well for ourselves," Kate answered.

"Are you happy?"

"Now, why would you ask me a question like that? Of course, I'm happy," she answered while poking him in the ribs.

"Just wanted to know," he said as he gave her a peck on the cheek. "Just wanted to know."

BUILDING A HOME

"We got it done, Pa," said Abraham as he stood back and admired their handiwork.

It had taken them two days to build the heavy wooden gate across the entrance to the cave. The gate guaranteed safety for the family. Angus had brought a heavy-duty set of hinges and a hasp from Tennessee. Thinking ahead, Angus had Atticus fire up his forge and blacksmith the hinges and the hasp into shape on his anvil. Now, taking a chain and a padlock, he locked the gate. Smiling, he turned to his sons.

"I've waited a long time for that. It feels almighty good knowing we are behind a locked gate. Nobody can sneak up on us," he said as he unlocked and swung it open. "We'll lock the gate every night before we turn in."

"Pa, we almost have the steps into the wall. Come and see," beckoned Ansel.

The men had discovered a place where they could get easy access to the wall directly above the entrance to the cave. Using sledgehammers and chisels, the men chipped stairs into the solid granite. On top, a concealed guard shack was built and manned around the clock. A rope was to be stretched from top to bottom for a handrail. A cast iron bell was then strategically placed nearby. If danger came along,

BUILDING A HOME

they had a way of warning the family by ringing the bell.

Now, the men were able to go on to other projects.

Angus had chosen the site for the main ranch house. Sitting on a slight knoll, it overlooked a small stream and a grove of lodgepole pines. Barely a half-mile from the cave, it was within easy earshot of the bell. The men had cleared the brush out of the way. They had rolled stones into place for the foundation and began building the ranch house.

Everywhere you looked, the sights and sounds of construction could be seen and heard. The pounding of hammers intermingled with the rasping of crosscut saws added to the construction din. Bare-chested men hoisted logs into place, and lads gathered the mud and dry weeds for the chinking. Angus was in charge of making cedar shakes for the roof. They all looked for rocks for the chimney.

The men completed the main ranch house and admired their handiwork.

"Fine job, boys," gleamed Angus. "The nicest home we've ever owned. Ain't that right, Ma?"

Kate nodded with tears in her eyes. "Bonnie! Thank you, boys."

The next building to go up was the barn. It was big and spacious, perfect for the livestock. The men built a roomy bunkhouse after that.

"Atticus, your blacksmith shop is next. Have you picked a spot for it yet? You're going to build your cabin next to it, aren't you?" asked Angus.

"Yes, Pa. I want it built on the stream a couple of miles from here. Jennie and I found a place we love. There are plenty of trees to shield us from the west wind. A good place for a garden and raising lads and lasses."

Everyone pitched in to help with the blacksmith shop. By the end of the week, Atticus and his family moved in after a week of hard labor.

And so it went. One by one, the families chose their building site. Each one according to their family's needs. Abraham chose ground next to a gushing stream roaring out of the granite wall. He had plans for a grist mill. There were places where the soil was so rich and fertile that it would grow anything. He had plans for growing wheat.

As each homestead went up, the men went on to the next one.

Ansel loved horses. His plans were for a horse ranch. Ansel put his cabin close to a box canyon that he could use for a corral. Game trails were abundant. But most of all, he wanted to monitor the wild horse herd.

It took a summer of backbreaking labor. Angus called the family together when the last cabin stood tall.

"We have one more building to build," he said.

BUILDING A HOME

"What is it?" moaned Little Angus because he was tired. His job had been digging the privies. His hands, heavily calloused from using the shovel, were sore. The blisters had finally toughened up. He was eager to get rid of the shovel.

"It's the most necessary building of them all. We need a church. Abigail can teach the lads and lasses their school lessons there."

"I had forgotten about it," replied Abigail. She was the schoolteacher for the clan.

"We have to build," Absalom said. "We need to get busy."

Everyone pitched in, and it went up quickly. Angus insisted it was built near the ranch house for convenience since he was the preacher. They added a belfry and moved the alarm bell into it. Trying the bell, Angus spoke above the clamor.

"Now it feels like home. Praise God! We are home."

Bright and early on Sunday morning, Angus began ringing the bell. The family arrived, entered, and sat on the rough-hewn log benches.

Angus went forward. His Bible was in his hands. Looking out over his family, he began to cry.

Regaining his composure, he softly spoke. "I have waited many years for this, all of my family under one roof.

And especially in the presence of the Heavenly Father. I missed all of your childhoods. I wasn't there for your birthdays, nor was I there for your victories or defeats. I missed it all. I told myself I was doing it for you. I realize now that I was doing it for me. I was selfish. I ask that you forgive me, please."

Immediately, his family surrounded him. Not a dry eye anywhere.

"Pa, we know you were doing it for us. We knew you did what you did with one thought in mind. Yes, we would have liked to have seen you more. But we understand and love you for it," offered a teary-eyed Ansel.

Wiping the tears from his eyes, he whispered, "I have a bonnie family, and I love you."

Later that night, Angus and Kate talked. It was something they always did before going to sleep.

"Not many would have done what you did. Behind that wall you have built is a sensitive, loving man, and I love you for it," Kate offered. "You showed the family a side of you they very seldom see."

Sobbing, Angus whispered, "My bonnie Kate, what would I do without you?"

She took him into her arms and prayed for him. It was the right thing to do. She was sure of it.

EXPLORING THE GLEN

The snow had melted to the point there were dirty, splotchy patches scattered about the cave entrance. The sun was a bright yellow orb in the sky, and a warm breeze came wafting in from the southwest. Everyone was sick and tired of winter, finding any excuse to leave that dank cave.

Angus stood at the cave entrance and stared off into the distance. The wanderlust spirit he had set in again, and it troubled him. It was something Angus had always had to deal with. Making up his mind, he turned and went hunting for his boys. Finding them at the cooking fire, he spoke.

"It's time we did some exploring. Only half of you can go this time. Ansel, Abner, Atticus, and Little Angus, saddle your horses. The rest of you can go another time. There's no way we can explore it all today."

They rode out midmorning. They were well-armed, and the women had packed vittles for two days.

"We may stay out overnight. Don't worry about us. We'll be back," Angus told Kate.

"Old man, you be careful out there," she admonished while giving him a peck on the cheek.

He smiled, nodded, and rode off.

"We need to see if there are any more entrances into

the glen. We need to find all the water holes and hunting areas. We might even look for gold. You never know what you'll find," he shouted as they rode.

The first place they stopped was the lake. They split up and began their search. There were wild game tracks everywhere. They saw elk, bison, and bear prints leading in all directions. The most intriguing thing they saw was the unshod horse tracks.

Reuniting, they shared what they had seen.

"Indians? We saw pony tracks on the other side of the lake," said Abner.

"I don't think so. Do you remember the first time you saw the valley? Remember seeing a small herd of wild horses? I think that is what those tracks are," answered Angus.

"Do you think we can catch them?"

"I don't know. But I do know this—we're going to try."

They all dismounted and went to the waterfall that was feeding the lake. Cupping their hands to catch the water, they drank long and deep.

"Sweet water!" exclaimed Atticus as he dried his mouth on his sleeve.

Angus smiled and said, "Aye, it is at that. Let's see if we can find some more. We need another source when we move the herds from graze to graze. It gives the grass a chance to recover."

As they rode, they marveled at the granite boundary walls. Tall and majestic, they were the perfect natural fencing. Not only to protect them but also to contain their cattle and horses.

"Look! Pa! Elk!" shouted Little Angus.

Ahead of them, they could see several elk running away from them. None of the elk had antlers because they had shed them going into spring. Chances were there were a couple of bulls in the group, but they couldn't tell for sure.

They watched as a bald eagle soared overhead and were amazed as they saw it dive down and snatch up a rabbit. It made a beeline for a high rocky promontory.

"It's heading for the nest," chuckled Angus. "Its missus is probably waiting on it."

Going on, they watched a herd of antelope race across the valley, the sunlight bouncing off their sleek, brown backs.

"Boys! There's food here aplenty. We won't starve. All we have to do is harvest it," Angus said as he watched the antelope. "The hardest will be the pronghorns. They're a mite skittish."

Up ahead, they saw a shadow on the granite wall. As they got closer, the shadow turned into a small box canyon.

EXPLORING THE GLEN

They saw a small stream fed by another waterfall cascading from a fissure in the granite. A large stand of pine trees shadowed the water. They estimated it was eighteen miles from the cave.

"This is perfect. We'll cut the timber and fence it. We can also build a line shack. We can brand our cattle and hold them in the canyon until we move them. It makes a great holding pen," added Angus. "Let's go farther."

Nothing new was clear until they were about thirty miles out. Little Angus was the first to spot it.

"Pa, take a look over yonder. See that dark spot in the wall? What do you reckon it is?"

"I'm not sure. Let's check it out," Angus answered.

The closer they got to the dark spot, it was apparent it was a hole. It was smaller than their cave entrance. But it was a good-sized hole. Game and horse tracks were everywhere.

"This may be another way in," Angus said as he dismounted and tied his horse to a pine tree branch. "Follow me and have your rifles ready. Bears love caves. I don't want to run into a grumpy grizzly."

They tied an old rag to a broken branch and made a torch. Lighting it, they ventured into the cave. As they rounded a bend, the cave opening was ahead of them. They stepped out into a small clearing surrounded by trees. Game trails came from all directions, merging into the clearing.

"I wonder how many more places like this there are? We need to find all of them. Decide which ones to keep open and which ones to close up."

"Why, Pa? Why do you want to close them?" asked Ansel.

"It's simple. In the future, when this wilderness is full of settlers, we may have a problem with rustlers. We need to control the valley the best we can," he answered, "not give them easy access to our herds."

The boys saw the logic and agreed.

"We'll go a little farther and camp. Head back tomorrow."

They went another twelve miles and found a stream gushing from the rocks. Setting up camp in a grove of trees, they got their supper ready. Later, Angus pulled his pipe from his pocket and lit it.

"I'm happy with what we found today. And we've seen only a wee part of it. I'm excited about our future here. What do you think about—"

Suddenly, they heard a commotion among their horses. They had hobbled them so that they couldn't get far. They heard nickering and neighing. As they rose to their feet, a shrill squeal split the air.

"A stallion! He's after the mares! Hurry, or we'll have a long walk back!"

They ran to their horses in time to scare the stallion away. In the dusk, they could see him. A magnificent animal, he was solid black and huge. The black stallion was one of the grandest horses they had ever seen. He raced away, turned, reared up on his hind legs, and issued a challenge. Then he was gone. They could hear the sounds of running hoofbeats in the distance. They listened until the sounds faded into silence.

"That's going to be our next task. We have to catch the black stallion and his mares. If we don't, none of our horses are safe," grumbled Angus. "There has to be a way we can catch him."

"Magnificent animal!" said Abner.

"What are we going to do with him?"

"Breeding. He'd be perfect for our horse ranch. The first horses came over with the Spaniards centuries ago. Many escaped, and their offspring survived and have reproduced for years. That's what these animals are," he answered, "but first, we have to catch them."

"Can we?"

"I don't know, but we're going to try!"

"Amen! Let's do it!"

"In due time, boys, in due time. Let's get back. I got me some thinking to do."

The next night, while lying in Kate's arms, Angus told

her about what they had seen.

"It sounds bonnie! I wish I could have seen it," she sighed.

"Kate, how long has it been since you rode a horse?"

"I don't rightly remember. Why?"

"If you're not used to a saddle, forty miles is a long way to ride."

"Do you reckon you could get a wagon out of the cave and into the glen?"

The ensuing silence was her answer. It was all right. Just listening was exciting enough. Rolling over, she closed her eyes and smiled.

"Good night, you old coot."

"Good night, my bonnie lass."

INDIANS!

"Indians!" shouted Abner as he raced into the cave. "They're coming up the river!"

"How many?"

"Seven or eight canoes. Maybe thirty men," he answered.

"Grab your rifles. Who knows what they are up to? You can never outguess an Indian," ordered Angus.

The men went to the cave entrance and spread out. Finding shelter behind the rocks, they watched as the first canoe stopped mid-river. The Indians studied the shoreline. Seeing wagon wheel tracks and hoofprints, they pulled to shore. As each canoe appeared, it did the same as the previous. Angus counted as they left their canoes.

"I count twenty-six," said Angus.

"So do I," offered Absalom. "What are we going to do?"

"We wait them out. Let them tip their hand. I've dealt with a lot of Indians before. One minute they want to trade and the next they're lifting your hair. We have to be careful. If they think they can overrun us, they will. They respect courage, so do your best not to show fear," replied Angus.

"Look, Pa!" Atticus said while pointing a finger.

Angus reared up and watched as an Indian cautiously

INDIANS!

stepped from behind a rock. He raised his hand toward them and waited.

"He wants to parlay. Cover me. I'll go see what he wants."

"Pa, are you sure? It might be a trap!"

"We have to take a chance. If we're going to live here, we must get along with them."

Angus slowly went to the river, watching for any signs of danger.

The Indian, using his hand as a visor, peered at him for a couple of minutes.

"Ahhngus!" he shouted.

Angus stared long and hard and then smiled.

"Beaver Tail!" he returned the shout. "You old fool! Is it you?"

"Ahhngus!" again came the call.

Angus turned, looked back at his boys, nodded, and went to the Indian. He grabbed him, picked him up off his feet, and gave him a tremendous bear hug.

"What in the world?"

"What's he doing?"

"I don't know, but keep your rifles ready just in case."

Angus and the Indian came arm in arm back to the cave. The braves followed them at a distance.

"Boys, this here is Beaver Tail. He's from the Nez Perce

tribe, and he's my friend. I met him when I was trapping this area. I found him in a bad way. A grizzly had got a hold of him. I nursed him back to health, took him back to his village, and we've been friends ever since."

"Do you trust him?"

"Boys, I trust him with my life."

Angus sat down on a rock and began talking in sign language with him. It seemed like hours had gone by before they finished talking. Finally, Angus stood up and spoke to his sons.

"I think we're all right. Beaver Tail has become the chief of his village. I told him about the valley and how much I loved it. I told him about you and what our intentions are. I asked him if we could live here in peace. If we can be good neighbors."

"What did he say?"

"He said he would have to take it before the tribal council. I'm going back to his village with him tomorrow."

"We're going with you! You're not going alone!"

"No, I have to go alone. It shows signs of bravery."

"Tell the women to fix plenty for supper. We have to feed them. You've never seen anybody eat until you see what they can pack away. It'll downright flamboozle you!"

And it did. It seemed as if each brave had a bottomless pit for a stomach. The boys couldn't believe it.

"Where did they put it all?" they asked each other. "They ate enough for a hundred men!"

At daybreak, Angus left with Beaver Tail and his braves. Before leaving, he called his sons aside.

"Ansel, you're in charge. I've told your ma not to worry, but you know she will. She always has and always will. Keep an eye on her."

"I will," he responded.

"Keep them busy. I'll be back soon."

He was gone for a week. A sigh of relief left the boy's lips as he stepped ashore. They quickly surrounded him, asking a thousand questions.

Raising his arms for silence, he spoke.

"If it weren't for Beaver Tail, we'd be dead. Most of the council wanted to send a war party after us. Beaver Tail told them about me helping him after the grizzly attack. Some of the elders remembered me, and that's what saved us. The valley is ours."

Shouts of excitement were long and loud. Again, Angus quieted them down.

"I made Beaver Tail a promise, and we'll keep it. We'll help them whenever we can. Once the herd is here, we'll supply them with beef. If they are sick, we'll nurse them. We'll become good neighbors, and they'll watch over us. They'll keep the other tribes at bay."

And so their relationship began. An Indian would drop off an elk carcass, and in return, the McDougals gave the Indians whatever they desperately needed. They were safe as long as Beaver Tail was alive and was chief. It was a good relationship for both sides. It was comforting to know they didn't have to worry about Indians. Little did they know what the future would bring and what they would have to do for their red friends. Little did they know.

CHRISTMAS

Winter hit early, and it struck with a vengeance. Angus had them prepared for it. From past experiences, he knew how harsh the land was. Their horses and cattle needed shelter from the elements. They had built corrals and sheds for that purpose. Tall grass had been cut and stored away for feed. The corrals were very close to a small spring. A small cabin had been built between the two corrals where they took turns spending the night watching the livestock. They had seen bear tracks in the area. With no way of replacing their animals, they couldn't take any chances.

The men had blocked off the cave entrances to ward off the cold. The women took some of the canvas wagon coverings and sewed them together, and the men built frames that fit the openings. The wagon covers were attached, and they kept most of the cold out. They had snaked downed trees into the cave and cut them for firewood. The wood was then neatly stacked throughout the cave. In a corner was a large pile of buffalo chips the lads had gathered. If they ran out of firewood, they could burn the chips.

The men had started hunting and had killed numerous elk, bison, and bears. On the drying racks, jerked meat was then stored for further use. In a far corner, the men had hung quarters of elk and bison. It was the coldest part of the cave, and it kept the meat ready for use. The women had taken the bear fat and rendered it into candles. The things they lacked were flour, sugar, and coffee. They wouldn't starve, but their diet was limited.

"What I wouldn't give for a hot cup of coffee," moaned Atticus.

"I want one of Ma's biscuits."

"Something sweet! It's all I can think about," complained Little Angus.

Christmas was right around the corner. The men had found a fine pine tree to make a Christmas tree for the lads and lassies. They made a stand for the tree and set it close to the cooking fire. The children had made ornaments out of anything they could find. Using scraps of cloth, they made pretty bows and carved crosses out of wood and anything shiny.

"I'm missing a pair of long underwear! Has anybody seen them?" asked Abner. "They're my favorite pair."

"Are they red?"

"Yes. Why?"

"Look at the tree."

Abner looked and saw the tree covered with red flannel stars. Turning to the wee ones, he asked, "Who did it?"

They smiled and went about what they were doing.

The grownups who had witnessed it howled with laughter.

"Going to get a mite drafty this winter!"

"Are you going to sew the stars back together again?"

"This I have to see!"

Abner muttered to himself and stormed away. Next time, he'd keep a closer watch on his belongings.

Meanwhile, at the table, Angus and Kate were huddled together.

"Angus, are you sure about this?" asked Kate.

"Aye, I'm sure. It's Christmas. We have to do something for the lads and lasses," he answered.

"Angus, you're a bonnie man," she smiled as she kissed him.

Ever since they had left Tennessee, he had been sneaking sugar from the barrel and stashing it away. He knew Christmas was a happy time. As far as he was concerned, the lads and lassies would have Christmas.

He enlisted his four daughters to help. Angus gathered them together and told them what he had done and what he intended to do.

"Pa! You old rascal! How long have you been doing it?"

"Ever since we left Tennessee."

"How much do you have?"

"By my reckoning, close to ten pounds," he answered.

"We can make the lads and lasses some candy. But we have to do it secretly."

"By the looks of the sky, I believe it will snow tonight. Maybe we'll get enough snow that they can play in it tomorrow. I'll keep them busy if you can get the candy made."

"It will be hard because we have to stir it. All I can say is that we'll try. We need a little molasses to go in it. Can you find us some?"

"I think I can come up with some. Since we can't make biscuits, we don't need molasses for them. I'm sure somebody's got some. Don't worry. I'll get it."

True to his word, he returned with a little brown jug.

"Where are you getting all of this? What else do you have hidden away?"

Ignoring the question, he said, "This is all there is. Use it sparingly, please."

That night, a foot of wet snow fell. It was perfect for a snowball fight.

After breakfast, Angus called all the lads and lasses together.

"I bet you can't hit me with a snowball!"

"I can!" they all squealed.

"I don't think so!" he teased.

"Let's find out," one of the boys challenged.

While Angus was getting massacred, the girls made the candy. While mixing the contents in large wooden bowls, the ladies saw what the girls were doing and joined in to help.

"Where did you get the sugar?" they asked. We thought we were out!"

"Angus has been stashing it away for Christmas."

"Bless his ornery old soul," they giggled.

Christmas morning came. After breakfast, Angus called them all together. He retrieved the family Bible, found his rocking chair, and began reading the story of Jesus's birth. As he read, there was silence. They could hear the wind howling outside, and the sound of it made them get as close to the fire as possible.

The hired hand, who had spent the night watching the stock, came in and warmed himself by the fire. He joined them. Even the guards left their posts and listened.

After finishing reading the scriptures, Angus began to pray.

"Heavenly Father, on this Christmas morning, in our new home, we celebrate the birth of Jesus. We thank You for sending Him to us as a way for us to attain Heaven. We thank You for the gift of Your Son. We thank You that You are watching over us. We ask that You continue to meet our needs and protect us. In Jesus's name. Amen."

Several repeated with "amen" as Angus finished his prayer.

With a twinkle in his eye, he motioned for his daughters to come to him. Each one was carrying a wooden bowl held high over their head.

"Lads! Lasses! Come to me, please," he beckoned. "Just as Jesus was a gift to us from the Father, this is a gift to you from your ma and pa."

Taking a bowl, he gave the hard-tack candy to the lads and lassies. Squealing with delight, they popped the candy into their mouths. There was enough left over that the adults enjoyed the sweet, wonderful candy.

Atticus fetched his violin and began playing "Silent Night." One of the brothers began singing, and soon everyone joined him. After finishing the song, they smiled and hugged each other.

"Merry Christmas, and may God bless you," beamed Angus. "Merry Christmas."

"I am so proud of you," murmured Kate as she nestled beside him. "You made Christmas special for the children."

"Did you see the look on Little Angus's face when he tasted the candy?"

"Yes. Little Angus has begged me for something sweet for a long time. He isn't much older than some of the lads and lasses. It made him feel special."

"Kate, my bonnie Kate, I have nothing to give you for Christmas," whispered Angus as he turned to face her.

"Nonsense! You gave me eleven children and a passel of lads and lassies. But most of all, you give me your love. That is the best Christmas gift you could ever give me," whispered Kate.

"I love you."

"I love you too."

They kept whispering this to each other until they fell asleep.

THE WEDDING

"Kiss your bride, son, kiss your bride!" Angus shouted with glee. "Constance, welcome to the family."

Family members gathered around the happy couple, clapping, shouting, and teasing.

"Alexander, you've got a pretty one. A bonnie lass, that's for sure."

Constance blushed and clung to Alexander's side.

Angus stood next to a group of people who were watching the proceedings.

"Well, Silas, it's done. They're hitched good and proper."

"I reckon they are, Angus. Thank you kindly. Take care of our Constance for us. Her ma and I are going to miss her."

"We will. I promise you that."

The past month's proceedings had been eventful. Angus remembered the day Absalom had raced down the steps from the guard shack and called him.

"Boat coming up the river!" he shouted.

"Gather your brothers. Let's see who they are. Make sure your brothers are armed. We can't take any chances," Angus had said.

They opened the gate and went to the river, arriving

about the same time the boat pulled to shore. Angus and his sons could see a handful of men peering at them from behind barrels and trunks. All the men aboard were armed and were watching them closely.

"Ahoy, the boat!" called Angus.

A man arose from behind a bale. He slowly worked his way to the stern, watching for any signs of danger.

"We're the Frasers. Who are you?" he asked.

"We're the McDougals. I'm Angus, and this is our place."

"We're looking for a place to settle. We're just passing through."

"Stop and rest a spell. We would welcome some company. Find out what is going on back east," offered Angus.

"Much obliged. Our women folk are tired of this old boat. They would welcome talking to yours," he replied.

"Come ashore. Your boat is safe here," offered Angus.

"Thank you, but I'm still going to post a guard," replied Fraser.

"Suit yourself. You're welcome here," said Angus.

The Frasers came ashore and followed Angus to the cave. Angus motioned for Ansel.

"Tell your brothers to keep an eye on them. We don't know these people. We aren't taking any chances," ordered

Angus in a whispered voice.

Ansel gathered his brothers, and the men talked for a few minutes.

"Follow me," offered Angus as he led them into the cave.

As they entered the cave, Fraser whistled softly in amazement. They walked past the wagons, past the fire where the women were preparing the meal, and out the glen entrance onto the bench.

Angus noticed the look on Fraser's face.

"We've laid claim on the whole valley. I discovered it back in '23 when I was with a trapping party. I put up my claim marker, and we recently returned."

"Indian trouble?" asked Silas Fraser.

"No, we have an understanding with them. We're good neighbors with the Nez Perce village," replied Angus.

"Unbelievable! I don't know how you pulled it off," returned Silas.

"It's a long story. I'll tell you later if we have the time," replied Angus.

"The valley is massive. Have any idea how big?" questioned Silas.

"I'm figuring it's around forty thousand acres. My sons and I explored it and have erected claim markers around the borders."

"What are your plans for it?"

"We want to run a large herd of cattle. See if we can't get a beef contract with Fort Hall. Also, we want a horse ranch. We plan to grow wheat for sure. Possibly corn, and we have plans for a grist mill. My son, Atticus, is a blacksmith. I'm sure that's not all we will do," answered Angus.

"You've done a lot of thinking about this place, haven't you?"

"Over twenty years worth, twenty-six years to plan, save money, and set aside provisions."

"I'm impressed. You've done well," said Silas.

"Thank you. Are you hungry? I imagine our women folk have supper ready. I'm sure there's enough for your family, too," offered Angus. "Go round them up."

"Don't mind if I do! Don't mind if I do!"

There were eighteen in Silas's family. There was Silas, his wife, Rebeccah, and their three sons with their wives and children. There was an unmarried son and daughter.

What caught the boys' eye was the daughter. She looked to be about sixteen. She had long blonde hair, blue eyes, and a slender frame. She was as cute as a button.

"Hey, Alexander," they teased, "will you look at that!"

"Isn't she pretty? Too pretty for you!" his brothers teased.

"Alexander, you better get her before Little Angus does!"

"Lay off, or I'll get you!" Alexander threatened.

During supper, he glanced at her. She returned the look and smiled. At that moment, he was in love. If a man could be in love without ever speaking a word to a girl, he was. After supper, Alexander worked up enough courage to approach her.

"Get enough to eat?" he said, feeling like a fool. He had no experience talking to a female and didn't know what to say.

"Yes, I did, Alexander," she said with a smile.

"Who told you my name?" he asked. "What's yours?"

"One of your brothers," she replied. "My name is Constance."

"Which one? I'm going to kill him!" Alexander said while looking at his brothers.

He could see them over in the corner, laughing and pointing their fingers at him.

"What else did my brother tell you?"

"That you're not married," she smiled.

"Now I know I'm going to kill them!" Alexander said out loud.

"It's all right. Will you show me the valley?" asked Constance.

THE WEDDING

"Do you want to see it?"

"Yes, I heard my pa tell my ma it was wonderful."

"It is. Here, let me help you up," replied Alexander as he took her hand.

It was dusk, and the moon was on the horizon. They heard a coyote's howl as they stood on the bench and looked over the valley. Alexander could sense that they weren't alone. Out of the corner of his eye, he could see one of her brothers and one of his.

"We have a chaperone," he whispered.

"What is a chaperone?" she whispered back.

"Someone to watch us. Make sure we don't do something we shouldn't," answered Alexander.

Giggling, she leaned over and gave him a peck on the cheek. "That will give them something to talk about."

"Why did you do that?" asked an astonished Alexander.

"I wanted to. I think you're cute."

Not knowing what to say, he motioned for her to follow him.

"We had better get back," Alexander quietly said.

That night was the worst night Alexander had ever had to endure. His brothers and sisters teased him without mercy.

"When are you getting married?"

"Ready for your chivaree?"

"Leave me alone," he had shouted.

From that moment on, Alexander and Constance were together. Wherever Constance was, you would find Alexander. It was so obvious it began to bring up questions.

As time flew by, Angus and Silas knew something needed doing.

"Silas, we need to talk," Angus said as they sat by the fire.

"I do believe we do," replied Silas.

"Are you all right with this thing between our children?" asked Angus.

"I believe so. We are fond of Alexander. I'm still trying to get around the notion of him being my son-in-law. Constance's mother is the one unsure about it. What do you think?"

"Alexander's mother and I feel the same. We like Constance and would welcome her into the family. What do we do?" questioned Angus.

They looked at each other and nodded. "Wait it out."

Within a couple of weeks, Alexander found Silas working on their boat. He approached Silas, hat in hand, and spoke.

"Sir, can I talk to you?"

Knowing what was coming, Silas answered, "What is it you want to talk about?"

"Sir, it's about Constance. Sir, I love her. We'd like to get married. I'm asking for your permission," said Alexander.

"I see. I've been watching both of you. It's for sure Constance loves you. Her mother and I have talked. We've never stood in the way of our boys and their wives. Will you take care of her?"

"Yes sir, the best I can," answered Alexander.

"That's all I need to know. You have my permission," smiled Silas.

Alexander took off, stopped mid-stride, turned, and yelled, "Thank You!"

Silas chuckled and went back to his work. He couldn't help but think back to when he sparked Rebeccah.

Alexander found Constance and told her. The happy couple shared the news. Their parents made the wedding plans. They set the date for a week later.

There was a quiet ceremony. Constance was escorted to his pa and Alexander by her pa as Atticus played his violin. And now he was urging Alexander to kiss his bride.

Alexander kissed Constance with a kiss, soft and sweet. The brothers and brothers-in-law congratulated them with hugs and backslaps.

The women had prepared a feast. Silas found a jug of corn squeezings. He passed it around until the men tasted

McDougal's Glen

the homemade liquor. Little Angus choked and gagged on his taste of it.

"Mighty fine, Silas, mighty fine," said Angus. "First snort I've had in many a moon. I don't normally imbibe, but this being what it is, I will make an exception."

"Will there be a shivaree tonight?" Silas wanted to know.

"Does a bear live in the woods? Course there will be," answered Angus.

"Good. I remember ours. Don't seem right not having one when you get hitched," answered Silas.

"We'll be there," Angus replied. "Still planning on pulling out the first of the week?" he asked.

"I believe so. You found yours, and I'm aiming to find mine. My land is out there somewhere, waiting for me to find it. I've got the itch to go," Silas said with a faraway look in his eye.

"I know the feeling. Thank the good Lord, I've cured my itch. We're going to miss you," said Angus.

"We're going to miss you, too. We'll let you know where we are. I imagine there will be a grandbaby one of these days," smiled Silas.

"Reckon a shivaree will prolong that wait?"

"Time will tell."

"C'mon, we've got a shivaree to go to," the two fathers

said as they put their arms on each other's shoulders.

Later, as Angus snuggled with Kate, he spoke.

"Silas and his family are leaving the first of the week."

"I was expecting it," answered Kate.

"Silas said he would let us know where they are. Also said they want to know when there is a bairn."

"What did you say?"

"I said I would. We also need to think about going to visit."

"I agree. Aren't you forgetting something tonight?" Kate asked.

"No, Kate, I haven't forgotten."

Closing his eyes, he began, "Father, I ask that you bless Alexander and Constance. Watch over them, keep them safe, help them get used to each other, and bless them. In Jesus's name, Amen."

THE SUPPLY RUN

"Pa, we need supplies. We're out of flour, coffee, sugar, and bacon—pretty much everything," said Ansel.

"I know. What are you thinking?" asked Angus.

"I'm thinking about taking Abner and Absalom and going after supplies. We won't last until spring if we don't. I was thinking about trying for Fort Hall. What do you think?" asked Ansel.

"It's worth a try. You'll need three good pack horses. I'll get you some money. When are you pulling out?"

"At first light."

The brothers left right after breakfast. Angus had given them a thousand dollars in gold. Ansel put it in his saddlebags, waved goodbye, and they were off.

"Be careful, boys!" Angus had called as they rode out of sight.

After eight days, he began to worry. They should have been back by now. They were a little over a hundred miles from Fort Hall. He was on the verge of going after them when they returned. He met them at the cave entrance.

"Where have you been? Get the supplies? Where are your horses?"

"Pa, we got robbed!"

"What happened?"

THE SUPPLY RUN

"We were within sight of the fort when we got jumped. There were six men. They came out of nowhere with their rifles on us. They took everything—our horses, rifles, and money. We didn't have a chance," offered a foot-sore and dejected Ansel. "It was a long walk home."

"Get something to eat. I know you're hungry. Then get some rest. Do you think you can identify the men?"

"Yes, I'm pretty sure I can," answered Ansel.

"We leave in the morning. Are you up for it?"

"I want my horse and rifle back. How's that for an answer?

"What I expected."

They pulled out early in the morning. Angus led them on at a hectic pace. Ansel, Absalom, Atticus, and Abner followed him cross country. He knew the lay of the land and instinctively knew shortcuts. In two and a half days, they were at the robbery site.

"Pa, this is the place," offered Ansel.

Angus dismounted and studied the terrain. It had snowed since the robbery, and the tracks had worn away.

"Let's go to the fort. Maybe we can find out something there," Angus suggested.

At the fort, they told the commandant what had happened.

"Six men, is that right?"

"Yes," answered Ansel.

"Can you identify them?"

"Yes, I'm sure I can," he answered.

"If they are here, they'll hang. Turn them over to me. I will have no vigilante justice here," the commandant threatened.

"We understand."

Outside the commandant's headquarters, they huddled and waited for Angus.

"What do we do?"

"There's a sutler's store on the post. You can learn a lot there. Keep your mouths shut and listen," said Angus.

They entered the store and separated. Angus went to the makeshift bar and gazed at the patrons. A smile crossed his face as he recognized someone.

"Whiskey Jack!" he shouted. "Is that you?"

The man looked up from his drink, stared long and hard, and answered, "Preacher?"

"It's me! How long has it been?"

"Over twenty years. What are you doing here?"

"We've homesteaded about a hundred miles from here."

"What are you doing at the fort?"

"My boys came after supplies and got robbed. We came back to find the skunks!" answered Angus.

THE SUPPLY RUN

"How many were there?"

"Six. Have you seen anybody like that?"

"Matter of fact, I have. Their leader is a man they call Rattlesnake. They're a pretty rough bunch."

"Know where they went?"

"I've got a good idea. The polecats like to watch the trail, always looking for easy pickings."

"Feel like having some fun?" asked Angus.

"Sure. It's been a while since I was in a ruckus."

"Can you take us to them?"

"I believe so."

"Let's go. Times a-wasting."

They left the fort and began their search. Whiskey Jack left the trail and rode a ridge parallel to it. About seven miles out, they saw smoke on the horizon. Getting close, they dismounted and began stalking through the trees. A campfire came into view with several men lying around it.

"Ansel, is it them?" asked Angus.

"I believe so, but I need a better look."

"Let's get closer."

The men crept toward the camp and surrounded it.

Angus hailed the camp. "Hands where we can see them! We've got you surrounded!"

What happened next was savage. The robbers grabbed their rifles and began shooting at them. Angus and his sons returned fire, and it was over in moments. Three of the gang were dead, two were wounded, and their leader was standing with his hands up.

"What do we do with them?" asked Ansel.

"If we take them to the fort, it'll be our word against theirs. We might be held responsible for this," answered Angus.

"I've got some rope," offered Whiskey Jack.

Angus looked at him and shook his head. "All we want is what is ours. You can have the rest."

They gathered their horses and rifles, and in Rattlesnake's saddlebags, they found most of their money. Rifling the dead men's pockets, they found enough to compensate for their loss.

"Whiskey Jack, are we square? Are you satisfied?"

Angus, with his Bible in his hand, approached the outlaws.

"Men, you're about to meet your Maker. You can do it on good terms or bad. Jesus loves you and wants you to allow Him into your hearts. Will you repent of your sins?" asked Angus.

"Old man, you can go to Hell!" snarled Rattlesnake.

Angus nodded and turned to Whiskey Jack. "I tried. They are yours."

Whiskey Jack nodded in agreement, and they left him

to take care of the robbers.

Later, at the sutlers, they loaded their supplies and started for home. They all kept quiet as they passed a tree with six bodies hanging from its branches. Angus offered a soft prayer as they rode down the trail.

"Pa, why did Whiskey Jack do it?"

"It's called frontier justice. Get used to it. We live in a savage land with savages living here. Don't you ever forget it!"

"Yes, Pa."

Kate was waiting for them when they got back. She had a relieved look on her face.

"Any trouble?" she asked.

The look on Angus's face was all it took.

Later, as they were lying in bed, she rolled over and took his hand.

"Well? Are you going to tell me or not?"

"Kate, we killed six men. We had no choice. There was a gunfight, and it was bad. We killed three outright, two were wounded, and the leader wasn't hurt."

"You said that six died?"

"If we had taken them to the fort, it would have been our word against theirs. Ansel identified them, so we knew they were the ones."

"So you hung them?"

"Whiskey Jack was with us. Do you remember him?"

"No, but go on."

"He did the hanging. We were able to get what was ours back."

"Did the boys see it?"

"No, but they did see the bodies hanging in the trees."

"Were you able to lead any of them to the Lord?"

Angus began to cry. "Kate, they wouldn't listen to me. I tried. The Lord knows I tried."

"Then their destiny isn't on you. The Lord knows your heart," she said as she held him in her arms. "He knows you tried."

"Pray with me, please," he whispered.

As the peace of the Lord settled over them, they fell asleep in each other's arms.

TRADING POST

The territory was beginning to fill up with settlers. Traffic had increased on the river considerably, and people were stopping all the time for information about the river ahead of them.

On the first day of April, Angus called a family meeting, "Something has been on my mind," he said. "It's time we made a few changes."

"Like what, Pa?"

"We're getting a lot of people coming through here now. Many of them didn't prepare as well as they should have. I was thinking about taking advantage of it. I reckon we should build us a trading post."

"Now, that's an idea!"

"Who would run it?"

"When do you want to do it?"

"Now, slow down. You know this is a family matter, and we'll have to vote on it," he answered.

"I have some questions. Where would we get our supplies?"

"That's a good question. I'm figuring we could haul it in from St. Louis. We still have our wagons, so that's no problem," answered Angus.

"What are we going to use for money? It's not going

to be cheap."

"I've been thinking about that also. We've got a passel of furs ready. I've got some gold stashed away. And there's something else."

"Pa, what are you thinking about?"

"If we take all our wagons, things will be discarded along the trail from here to St. Louis. We can scavenge along the way. Goods we can't sell here we haul to town and trade them for what we need. We'll stash and pick up the goods we can use on the way home."

"Makes sense."

"Let's take a vote."

The vote passed almost unanimously, and the discussion continued.

"Pa, what's our next step?"

"I figure we need to make the trip as soon as possible. It will take us a minimum of four and a half months to make the trip. But first things first, we need to build the post. The weather has broken, and hopefully, winter is over. We start tomorrow."

After five weeks of back-breaking labor, Angus and the men stood back and admired their handiwork. They had built a small pier and dock that led to a large log building on the river's bank. A sign above the door said, "McDougal's Trading Post." Off to the side was another

McDougal's Glen

log building for storage and stables.

"Pa, it's just what we need," offered Little Angus.

You're right, son. It's been a long time coming," answered Angus. "It will do us mighty fine."

"When do you want to leave?" asked Ansel.

"Today's Tuesday. We leave on Saturday. It gives us a day to rest and two days to get the wagons across the river."

"Who goes and who stays behind?" asked Absalom.

"Twenty-eight wagons, extra horses, and outriders will go. I'm figuring forty-eight of us plus your ma. That will leave the hired hands here to take care of things," answered Angus.

"So, all of us get to go?" asked Little Angus.

"Yes, but don't pester me about it!" glared Angus.

"We leave like I said, we should be back by October. That is, if we don't have any trouble. We have to get back before the snow hits us. If we bust our tails, we can do it."

They got the wagons across the river with little difficulty, and Saturday morning, they pulled out.

Angus instructed the foreman about what needed to be taken care of while they were gone.

"If we're not back by the first of November, you had better come looking for us."

The foreman nodded and shook Angus's hand. "We'll

take care of the place and your families."

"That's all I ask," said Angus, while pulling away from the river.

On the fourth day out, the party began finding things discarded along the trail. There was a trunk of clothing, dishes, a grandfather clock, buckets, and tools. They found practically anything you could think of if you looked long enough.

"Pa, we need this anvil," called Absalom.

"You're right. Let's stash it somewhere. We'll pick it up on the way back."

Finding an outcropping of rocks, they hid the anvil and other things. Marking the spot, they went on.

By the end of two weeks, they had three wagons full of goods for the trading post. The most important things they found were three barrels of gunpowder and a dozen rifles.

When the group stopped to camp that night, Angus called another meeting.

"I think we had better split up."

"Why, Pa?"

"It makes no sense driving three wagons full of trading post goods to St. Louis and back. I'm thinking about five wagons heading for home tomorrow. We can fill the empty ones with the goods we've stashed. Six men to go along as mounted security. What do you think?" asked Angus.

"Who goes on, and who turns back?" asked Atticus.

"Ansel, I'd like you to take charge of the return party. I know you wanted to see St. Louis, and I'm sorry, but I think this would be our best option. We'll draw straws to see who goes on and who goes home. That will be fair for everyone," answered Angus.

As usual, Little Angus drew a short straw and was in the return party.

"Pa! I wanted to go with you! It's not fair!"

"Hush up, boy. You drew that straw fair and square."

Little Angus hushed up and went off to pout by himself.

"Ansel, I'm counting on you. I want you to be ready for us when we get back."

"We'll be ready. Don't worry," answered Ansel.

At daybreak, they split up. Angus watched as they pulled out for home until he couldn't see them anymore. Turning back, he motioned for his party to leave. They filled several of their remaining wagons with discarded things to trade. They were able to stash more for the return trip along the way.

"Did you see the look on Little Angus's face?" asked Kate. "All he's talked about was seeing St. Louis."

"I know. But drawing straws was the only fair way to do it. All of the return party wanted to see the big town. He's young. There will be other times when he can go," answered Angus.

"I know it, and you know it. The boy's feeling sorry for himself," said Kate.

"I'll make sure he gets to go the next time we need supplies."

"That would be nice," she said while nestling beside him on the wagon seat.

Pulling into St. Louis, they immediately went to a fur buyer.

"Hello, Angus! How long has it been?" asked an old acquaintance.

"It's been many a moon. We've got some prime pelts to sell. Interested?" asked Angus.

"I'm always interested. Let me see what you've got."

The buyer liked what he saw and made an offer, which Angus quickly accepted.

"What now, Pa?"

We need to find a mercantile where we can trade our goods. I know where to go. The best place in town is right down the street. I know the owner. I've done business with him before."

Arriving at the mercantile, Angus entered and spotted who he was looking for.

"Silas, you old goat!" he shouted.

The man looked up, stared, smiled, and returned the

greeting.

"Angus McDougal! You old bandit! What are you doing here?"

"We're looking to make a trade. We've got several wagons full of goods you can use."

"What are you trading for?"

"We're homesteading in Idaho on the Snake. Thinking about opening a trading post. We're here for goods to stock it."

"Well, let me see what you've got," came the reply from Silas.

Angus let him poke through the wagons. After Silas finished, he approached Angus.

"Where did you get all of this?"

"We found it along the trail. Can you use it?"

"I do believe I can. I recognize a lot of it. I sold it to the immigrants before they left town."

"What's it worth in trade?" asked Angus.

"Let me ponder on it for a few minutes."

"All right. While you're pondering, we'll look for what we need."

While Angus, Kate, and the men were looking, Silas and his assistants made a list of what was in the wagons. Finished, he approached Angus with a total.

"I'm figuring four thousand in trade."

"Sounds fair. I've got another thousand in gold to add to it. We'll start piling up goods."

Angus, Kate, and the boys got busy. The want list was enormous. They needed rifles, powder, flint, lead, knives, traps, blankets, winter coats, and hatchets. Kate was making her pile. She knew what the women needed. Flour, sugar, coffee, lard, salt, needles, thread, bolts of cloth, and soap were in her pile. She also cared for their feminine needs that the men would have forgotten. As the quantity grew, Silas kept a tally.

Angus approached him. "We need another wagon and team. Tell me when we get there."

Silas nodded in agreement and kept adding. By midday, he motioned for them to stop.

"Close enough, Angus. I even threw in a few extras. I know you're a God-fearing man, and I thought long and hard about this. I added five barrels of sour-mash whiskey. Where you are, a nip, when it's cold, goes a long way towards a man feeling warm inside. You should be able to sell it easily. It's a little incentive to make you return to me when you need more supplies. I'll even take your furs in trade. Sound agreeable?" asked Silas.

"Silas, you're a good man. You got yourself a deal," answered Angus as they shook hands to seal the deal.

"We'll be back next year. Watch for us!"

"Sure will. Have a safe trip."

It took all of Silas's men to load the wagons. They left town and camped a few miles out. Hank, one of the mounted men, drove the new wagon, his horse tied to the wagon.

"Well, boys, we did better than I thought we would. I hope Ansel was able to get what we stashed."

That night, as Angus and Kate got comfortable under the wagon, Angus spoke. "Did you get everything on your list?"

"I think so. The sad thing is, you always forget something," Kate answered.

"I know. But I did remember something," Angus said.

"What?"

"Remember Christmas and what we did?"

"What did you do?"

"Close your eyes and open your mouth," Angus said.

"Can I trust you?"

"Open your mouth."

Angus slipped a piece of hard candy into her mouth.

"Candy?" she smiled as she sucked on it.

"I bought a ten-pound keg of it. No more scrounging sugar and molasses!"

"The lads and lassies will love it!"

"So will Little Angus!"

"I know where to hide it."

"Good."

The return trip was uneventful, and the second week of October, they were sitting on the opposite side of the Snake from their home. Angus fired a shot to let the home folks know they were back.

In no time, help arrived, and they were safely across the river. All of them were exhausted. That evening, everyone gathered for a meal together, and with full bellies and happy hearts, they marveled at the amount of goods brought back. After that, they had gone home.

The following morning, it was hustle and bustle as they unloaded the wagons and began stocking the shelves. It was good that they did. While moving the last barrel, they couldn't help but notice a random snowflake in the air.

Exhausted again, all the men and women stood back and marveled at their hard work.

Angus couldn't help but shout with pride, "McDougal's Trading Post is open! Yessiree! Thank you, Lord!"

THE STALLION

"Pa, here he comes," whispered Ansel.

It was daybreak, and Angus, Ansel, and Abraham watched the lake from behind a pile of large rocks. They had gone into hiding earlier. They hoped the wait was going to pay off. Peering from behind the rocks, the men could see the horses coming. Leading the herd was the black stallion.

The black would stop, lift his nose, test the breeze, drop his head, and come closer. He had lived as long as he had by being wise and cunning. He was proving his leadership qualities now. Sensing it was safe to approach, he led his mares to the water.

"Get ready," whispered Angus. "We need those horses, especially the black."

As the horses drank, the men sprang into action. From their hiding place, they charged with lariats twirling overhead. The stallion saw them coming and squealed a warning. The herd immediately burst from the water, with the men in hot pursuit. They had watched the herd's patterns for weeks and knew where the horses watered and where they bedded down at night. Dividing up into teams, every man knew what they expected to do. Each team's job was to wear the horses down until they could capture the herd.

They drove the herd until dark, pushing them into a small box canyon. Abner, Alexander, and Absalom were there to meet them. They dragged brush across the canyon's entrance to contain the herd. The stallion was furious. He repeatedly charged the brush fence, would rear up, and squeal in defiance. The stallion and his mares paced the canyon all night, looking for a way out. The men had built bonfires along the brush wall to keep them in.

"It won't hold them. We'll have to do the same thing tomorrow night. Try to get some sleep," ordered Angus. "Abner, Alexander, Absalom, I want you, at first light, to head to the next canyon and get ready for us. We'll drive the herd there."

While eating their breakfast, they heard a crash and a squeal. Looking up, they saw the stallion tearing down the fence.

"Quick! Mount up!" ordered Angus.

The eight men had brought extra horses for remounts. They had brought the horses to the canyon the day before and had tied them off to pine trees. One of the hired hands stayed with the horses until they got there. There were mountain lions and bears in the area. They were ready for it when the stallion destroyed the fence. The black led the mares out, and the chase began again. The three brothers headed for the other canyon, leading the horses used the day before behind them.

By the end of the day, the mares were beginning to lag. They put up little resistance as the brothers roped them. The black stallion would squeal in defiance as he prodded along his dwindling herd of mares.

Abner handed the lead ropes to Atticus. The rest of them continued the chase. He tied the exhausted mares to a pine tree and sat on a rock.

"We'll be back. Stay put and build a fire," ordered Angus.

Angus, Ansel, and Abraham continued the drive, constantly pushing the stallion and his mares.

"I hope Little Angus is ahead with fresh horses," shouted Ansel.

He was, and Angus and his brothers made a fast swap.

"Meet us at the next canyon. Your brother should be there by now," shouted Angus as they sped away after the wild horse herd.

By nightfall, they had driven them to the next canyon. The horses had gone without water and were showing it. The herd was so tired they were able to rope them without difficulty. That is, all except the black. He fought them off. None of them could get close to him.

"Build a fire. I'm going after Atticus," ordered Angus.

They had driven the horses around the wall of the canyon. Atticus was straight across the valley. They could see a pinpoint of light that had to be his fire.

The men closed off the canyon while Angus was gone. A couple of hours later, he returned with Atticus and the captured mares. They had tied them off to their saddle pommels so they couldn't break free. As much as the horses tried, it was futile. The tame saddle horses wouldn't spook. Building several bonfires, they bedded down for the night.

"Little Angus, Alexander, Absalom, and Abner, take the horses back to the ranch tomorrow. It will take all four of you to handle them. We're going after the black," ordered Angus.

"Yes, Pa," they answered in unison.

Morning came, and the black stallion destroyed the fence again and took off. The men were expecting it and were ready. They knew he was thirsty and would try to head for water. There was a small box canyon ahead with a stream running through it. The black was finally slowing down. They were able to steer him into the small canyon.

"We've got him!" shouted Angus. "Quick! Block the canyon!"

They did so and watched the horse drink long and heavy from the stream.

"What do we do now?" asked Ansel

McDougal's Glen

"Build bonfires. Atticus, Abraham, I want you to stay at the mouth of the canyon. If he tries to escape, drive him back into the canyon. Understand?"

They nodded in agreement and got ready.

"Good! Ansel, you're with me. Get your lariat ready."

The men mounted and slowly stalked the black. The stallion saw them coming, reared up, squealed in hatred, laid its ears back, and charged them.

"Watch out!" shouted Angus as he threw his lariat.

Somehow, it found its mark, and Angus now had his hands full, trying to hold a 1,400-pound stallion. He quickly tied the rope to his saddle horn.

"Hurry, Ansel! Get a rope on him!"

After three tries, Ansel had him. Angus and Ansel spread out with the stallion between them, rearing and snorting with rage.

Atticus and Abraham came running.

"See if you can throw a rope on his front leg."

They both tried, and Atticus connected.

"We have to throw him. It's the only way we can control him. Atticus, Abraham, pull him down with that rope," shouted Angus.

They heaved until they got the stallion down. Angus jumped down and covered his head with a saddle blanket.

"Take that front foot and bend it upward. Be careful!

He'll kick the daylights out of you! Take another rope, tie it around his hoof, and throw it over his back. We're going to put him on three legs. When he gets up, we'll throw the other end of the rope around his hoof. Pull it tight, tie it off, and he can't run. We'll walk him home on three legs," ordered Angus.

They gave him some slack, and he got up. Abraham grabbed the other end of the rope. He and Atticus pulled until the horse was on three legs. They quickly looped it around his hoof, and they had him.

"Don't get too close! He'll take a hunk out of your hide!" warned Angus.

The boys heeded his warning and admired the strength and beauty of the stallion.

"He's magnificent!" marveled Angus.

"A true beast, he is," shouted Abraham.

"He'll sire many great horses for us," said Angus. "Let's get some sleep."

On the way home the following morning, Angus began to chuckle.

"Pa, what's on your mind?" asked Ansel.

"I was just wondering. Which one of you is going to break the stallion? It's not going to be me."

The boys looked at the stallion and each other.

Each one was muttering, "What have I got myself

into?"

When they got to the ranch house, Kate stood on the porch.

"Kate. Isn't he a beauty?" asked Angus.

At that moment, the stallion stretched out and bit a hunk out of Ansel's horse. It bolted and threw Ansel onto the nearby woodpile. He lay there and moaned.

Kate locked eyes with Angus until he had to look away.

"You had better shoot that monster!" she threatened. "If that brute hurts anymore of you, then you'll have me to deal with!" Then she stomped off into the ranch house.

Angus didn't know what to do. They needed the black for breeding. He also knew that when Kate was riled and had her Scottish blood boiling, he had better steer clear of her.

By bedtime, she had cooled down some. At least she let Angus get in bed with her.

Taking her hand in his, he whispered, "Kate, we need the black. He'll sire a lot of good horses. But we have to break him."

She glared at him. "Or he'll break you!"

"There are ways of breaking him without anyone getting hurt."

"There is?" she said, while watching him closely. She knew how to tell if he was stretching things a bit. "Swear on the Bible?"

"You'd make me do that?" he asked.

"What do you think?" she answered.

"Let me say this. I promise you nobody will get badly hurt," he answered.

"I guess I can live with that," she muttered. "I am glad you caught the black and the mares."

"We'll start breaking them tomorrow. Do you want to watch?"

His answer was silence, and he was relieved. He loved Kate and would do anything for her. Reaching over, he kissed her brow and went to sleep.

She wasn't asleep. She was praying for safety. She knew the men would need it.

BREAKING THE BLACK

Kate was taking a nap. She had pulled her rocker out onto the porch and had closed her eyes. She was jolted awake by shouting at the corral in the middle of a dream about her grandchildren. Standing up and using her hand as a visor, she stared in that direction to see Ansel fly over the fence and land in a heap.

"Land sakes!" she muttered as she headed toward the corral.

By the time she got there, Ansel was on his feet, but just barely. He wobbled over to the fence and leaned against a fence post.

"Nice try!" shouted Angus. "You stayed aboard for what? A buck and a half?"

Kate approached the corral and asked, "What in tarnation are you doing?"

"We are trying to break the black," answered Angus.

"Looks to me like you're trying to break your back," she snorted as she peered through the corral. The stallion had backed up against the fence. The black was trembling, eyes wide with rage and whistling in defiance.

"You're addle-headed!" she shouted. "Shoot that horse before it kills one of you!"

"We can't do that. That critter is the future of our horse

breeding," replied Angus.

Kate stared at him and walked away, muttering something about men being idiots.

"Who's next?" shouted Angus.

"I guess I'll give it a try," answered Atticus.

Angus could tell that he was afraid as he watched Atticus climb the fence and approach the horse. Even though four men were holding him, the black glared with hatred as Atticus neared. It flinched as Atticus mounted and then tensed up, just waiting to be released so that it could get this hated thing off its back.

Atticus nodded, and the men let loose. The black jumped straight up and twisted in midair and then barrel-rolled. Atticus somehow got free of the saddle and landed flat on his back. The horse got to his feet and came for him, ears laid back and showing its teeth. If it hadn't been for his brothers, it would have bitten Atticus.

"That was close!" Atticus muttered as he approached Angus.

"I guess I'm going to have to show you how to do it," laughed Angus.

"Pa, if we have to hog-tie you, you're not going to ride that beast!" shouted Ansel.

"I'm not?" answered Angus.

"No! You're not!" shouted the brothers in unison.

"I guess it's my turn," offered Abner.

He mounted the black and took a handful of the horse's mane. They turned him loose, and he stood stock-still. Abner looked at Angus and shrugged his shoulders. That's when the black exploded into action. With one mighty buck, he sent Abner flying over his head. Abner landed on his butt with a gasp of pain. That was the least of his worries. The black was on him instantly, biting his shoulder and rearing up as if to strike him with his hooves.

"Help him!" shouted Angus as he came off the fence.

One of the brothers had a rifle. He fired a round into the sky, and the black broke off the attack.

Abner was in bad shape when they got him out of the corral. He was bleeding, and his rump was hurting so badly he could hardly walk. They found a bench for him to sit on. He couldn't do it. His backside was killing him.

Angus went back to the corral and stared at the black. The horse defiantly returned the stare.

"So, you think you won!" he said. "We aren't done with you yet! Who else wants to try? Alexander, how about you?"

"Pa, you know I'm not a coward. I haven't lost all of my wits yet. That horse is not going to kick them out of me."

Angus stared at him and shook his head. "Well, I guess

it's my turn."

"No, Pa, you're not going to do it!"

"Then how are we going to get him broke?"

"I'm going to do it," shouted Little Angus.

"You? Have you gone plumb loco? That horse will eat you alive!" shouted Angus.

"Watch me!" he answered.

All of his brothers began chuckling and teasing him.

"Where do you want to be buried?"

"Sure hope Ma has a lot of bandages. You'll need them!"

"Can I have your hat? You won't need it anymore."

"Can you play a harp? I hear that's what they play in Heaven."

Ignoring his brothers, he entered the corral carrying a rope.

He climbed aboard and handed it to Ansel. "Tie my feet together under his belly. He can't buck me off," he ordered.

Angus saw what was happening and yelled, "What if he rolls with you? What you're doing is suicide!"

Now everyone was watching real close. What Little Angus was doing was dangerous.

Little Angus leaned over and bit the black's ear. Then he nodded for the men to let loose of the black. The black squealed in pain and took off, with Little Angus biting its ear. It couldn't buck the boy off because he was tied on, and its ear was hurting.

The black didn't try any of its usual tricks. All it could think about was its ear. It raced around the corral with Little Angus holding on for dear life. Little Angus loosened his grip on the stallion's ear whenever it slowed down. When it sped up, the boy bit down harder.

Finally, the black stopped, and Little Angus let go of its ear and sat up. He latched on to the stallion's ear again when it started running. He kept biting the black's ear until the horse was exhausted.

Little Angus let go and sat up during the last time around the corral. The black kept going and didn't try any tricks. After about ten laps, Little Angus reined him to a stop. Reaching down to rub his neck, he yelled, "Well, I guess he's broke."

Angus and the brothers were speechless. They had never seen anything like it before.

"Boy," said Angus, "if I hadn't seen it with my own two eyes, I wouldn't have believed it!"

The brothers began to shout. It startled the black, and off it went again. But Little Angus bit its ear until it quieted down.

Little Angus was the only man who could ever ride

the black. Anyone other than him would get bucked off immediately. His brothers were jealous, but he didn't care. It became his horse. Little Angus named him Banshee, and they bonded with each other. He could call the black, and he would come to him and eat out of his hand. Anyone else would probably lose a finger.

Little Angus became the man they turned to when a horse needed breaking. His teeth became a legend.

TRAGEDY ON THE RIVER

"Pa! Look up ahead!" shouted Abner over the roar of the river rapids.

Angus leaned over the side of the boat as directed. He could see what appeared to be wreckage along the riverbank.

"Pull in," he ordered, "but keep your eyes peeled. Sometimes it's a trick to draw us in close. Absalom, you watch those rocks over there. Any sign of trouble, you give out a yelp!"

The McDougal men had built a boat, and this was its maiden voyage. They had left early the previous morning to scout the river downstream from the glen. They had camped and were about twenty miles from home. It was mid-morning when Abner shouted.

"Easy now. We don't want to take any chances," Angus admonished. "Ma'd skin me alive if something happened to you."

"Yes, Pa," came the reply as they eased to shore.

Abner jumped out and steadied the boat. Angus, Absalom, and Little Angus scrambled out and ran for cover. Once in the safety of the large boulders, they hunkered down and talked.

"Abner, what did you see?" asked Angus.

"It looks like a raft or keelboat broke up on the rocks. I saw a trunk and a couple of barrels on the shore. I didn't see hide nor hair of any people or critters," answered Abner.

"We better have a look, see," said Angus. "Little Angus, you watch out. You see anything, fire a shot."

"Aw, Pa," he grumbled. "I want to go!"

A stern look from Angus shut him up.

They crept, Indian style, toward the wreckage. Angus sensed all was clear and motioned for Little Angus to join him.

"See any footprints?" asked Angus.

"No, but it rained a couple of days ago. Any footprints would be gone," answered Abner.

"Let's see what we can salvage. Make a pile by the boat. Little Angus, you keep an eye out," ordered Angus.

It was like a treasure hunt. The men found plunder along the bank for almost a mile. They found an iron kettle, steel traps, broken crockery, and a pouch of men's and women's clothes. There were two barrels. One of the barrels was full of flour. The other one was full of whiskey. The trunk was full of things belonging to a woman. There was a mirror, combs, and a bone-handled hairbrush, among other things. Absalom found a rifle on the river bottom.

"Look, Pa, it's a Sharps," he shouted while holding it up for all to see.

"Good! They're hard to come by," answered Angus.

"I found a sack of corn. Do you reckon the people had any critters with them?"

"Probably. Most people do that are homesteading."

"Wonder where they are?"

"They probably haven't wandered far. Abner, get up on that ridge and tell me what you see," shouted Angus.

Abner took his time and shouted, "I can see some hogs. I think there are four out there. Oh, I can see a cow and her calf. I don't see any horses," he called out.

"Let's see if we can round them up."

Herding scared hogs isn't easy. The men were tired by the time they had them corralled. The cow and calf were no problem. They threw a rope around her neck, and she followed them back to the boat.

"What do we do, Pa?" asked Little Angus.

"I've been thinking about it," he answered. "The only way we can keep them is if we go back for help."

"Who goes and who stays?" asked Absalom.

"Help me build a holding pen for the hogs. Then you and Abner head back. It'll take a while because you're going upstream. I figure it will take six days there and back. Bring a wagon, a team of horses, and saddled horses

TRAGEDY ON THE RIVER

with you. Oh, and tell your ma what's going on so she doesn't worry about us," he answered.

They built the holding pen. Absalom and Abner got ready to leave.

"Watch yourself," called Abner as they launched the boat.

Angus nodded and waved. He knew it was going to be slow and hard work rowing upstream. He and Little Angus kept scavenging the wreck site. They found a bag of shells for the Sharps, a small cask of gunpowder that was miraculously still dry, bars of lead, an anvil they couldn't get out of the river, and there was still more.

Weary, Angus started looking for a secure campsite. In among the rocks, he found a place to his liking. There was only one way in. It had a rock outcropping covering, was dry and defendable.

"We need some firewood. It's hard telling how long we'll be here until your brothers return," said Angus.

"Pa, we can burn the wreckage. It's good and dry," answered Little Angus.

Angus agreed with a grunt. He sat down on a rock and lit his pipe. While sitting there, he wondered what had happened. There were no signs of an Indian attack. No signs whatever that told him what had happened. Little Angus interrupted his thoughts by dropping a load of

McDougal's Glen

firewood.

"Get it going," said Angus. "I'll see about supper."

Before Abner and Absalom had left, they had divided the vittles between them all. Angus and Little Angus got most of it because they would have to wait until they returned. From the wreckage, they found a frying pan. While Little Angus was fetching more wood, Angus put on some bacon to fry. The aroma was like a magnet. It drew Little Angus back to camp.

"I'm starved! My belly's asking questions, and my mouth ain't answering it!" he moaned.

"Sit and eat."

While eating, the two talked.

"We better keep a watch tonight," said Angus. "I'll take the late one. I'm going to get some shut-eye. Wake me up if something doesn't look right."

It seemed like Angus had just shut his eyes when he felt a nudge. Instantly, he was awake, one hand on his rifle and the other on his knife. After living most of his life on the frontier, Angus had learned to be ready for anything. Seeing it was his boy, he relaxed his guard.

"It's past midnight, more like one in the morning. I can hardly keep my eyes open. I reckon it's your turn."

Angus rolled out of his blanket, grabbed his rifle, and took his place where Little Angus had been. He settled in with his back to the fire. He had learned that lesson long ago. The firelight played tricks on your eyes. He knew it for a fact. One of his best friends lost his life to an Indian because he didn't see him until he was on top of him. While sitting there, he could hear a coyote yodeling off in the distance. He had always enjoyed listening to them, and this was no exception. Other than the coyote, everything was quiet. He could hear the gurgling of the river as it cascaded over the rocks. It was a pleasing sound, one to relax a man.

Angus had been watching for what he figured was maybe a couple of hours. Then he heard it, the ever so slight sound of rustling. Coming instantly alert, Angus waited for it to happen again. He sat perfectly still for an eternity and then heard it again. This time, it was much closer. He didn't think it was an Indian. You didn't hear Indians until they were right on top of you, and besides that, they don't attack at night. It was something else.

"Cougar," he thought and then dismissed it. Most critters, other than coyotes, don't hunt at night. But what could it be?

Out of the corner of his eye, he caught the slightest movement. It got all of his attention. He didn't dare wake up Little Angus. He needed to know what he was facing. Where he was sitting, he was pretty well hidden. He didn't know if whatever it was knew where he was. One thing for

McDougal's Glen

sure, he wasn't taking any chances.

Suddenly, he saw it again. He saw movement in the shadows. He could tell it was coming toward him. He pulled his knife from its sheath and waited. As it got closer, he could make out the form of something crawling on all fours. He could tell it was small. He still wasn't sure what it was. It reached his hiding spot and was almost past him when he realized what it was.

"It's a lad!" he gasped.

Springing from concealment, Angus clamped a hand over its mouth and tried to subdue it. There was an immediate yelp of surprise, and the struggle began. Angus had a hold of a wildcat by the tail. The boy did everything he could to get loose, including kicking Angus's shins and biting his thumb. Angus gasped with pain and finally got the lad under control. The commotion woke Little Angus, and he came running.

"Whatcha got, Pa?" he whispered.

"I don't rightly know for sure. It does have a good set of teeth," he whispered. "Let's take it to the fire and see what we caught."

Little Angus threw some wood on the fire. It flared up to reveal a small boy. He was barefoot, his clothes were rags, and he had a terrified look on his face.

"If I turn you loose, stay put," ordered Angus. "We're

not going to hurt you. Are you hungry?"

The boy nodded, Angus let loose, and he jumped up to run. Angus was expecting it and grabbed him again.

"I know you're scared. We aren't going to hurt you. Son, put on some bacon to fry. A full belly takes care of all sorts of problems," he said while watching the lad closely.

The boy watched as Little Angus fried the bacon. Little Angus handed it to him, and he swallowed it in one gulp.

"Slow down! It'll make you sick!" ordered Angus. "What's your name? You were on that boat. Am I right?"

Big tears welled up in the lad's eyes, and he began to cry. Angus waited for the sobbing to quit.

"Lad, you can tell me. We want to help you."

"Zeke," he whispered. "Ezekiel Fisk."

"Zeke, can you tell me what happened?" asked Angus.

"At Fort Hall, the sutler told my pa about a place to settle. We were heading that way when we hit the rapids. Pa lost control, and we hit some rocks. I got thrown out of the boat and almost drowned. The last I saw of my family was the boat going sideways down the river," he said while sobbing.

"What did you do?"

"I started following the riverbank, looking for them. I found the wreckage just like you did. But I can't find my ma, pa, or sister, Sulie Jo. I don't know where they are," he began crying again.

Angus took the lad in his arms and held him tight.

"Lord," he silently prayed, "show me what to do and how to help him."

"Zeke, I sent my sons back for help. When they get back, we'll look for your family," said Angus. "That's the best we can do. Let's put you down for the night. We'll make a place for you by the fire."

They covered him with a blanket, and he went to sleep immediately. Come morning, they fried up some more bacon and got Zeke to tell them about himself and his family.

"We come from Kentucky. We tried to farm a patch that had more rocks than dirt. We were so poor we almost starved. Pa talked to a man in the local tavern. He told Pa about land free for the taking. All we had to do was come to Idaho. We packed up and came. All of our family is still in Kentucky."

"Where in Idaho?"

"The sutler told us a hundred and fifty miles up this river. Said we could get supplies from a trading post up ahead. We planned to stop, get some idea about what was ahead of us, and get supplies. Pa was out of chaw tobaccy, and Ma needed some sugar. We ran out a couple of weeks ago."

"Zeke, that's our place. We own the trading post. Our

name is McDougal. I'm Angus, and this is my son, Little Angus."

Zeke nodded and got quiet.

Angus and Little Angus left him to his thoughts.

"Pa, what do you think?"

"I think he's hurting something fierce inside for his ma and pa. It will take time for him to get over this. All we can do is wait and see what happens."

A week later, the wagon arrived. Ansel had come along with them.

"What took you so long?" yelled Angus.

"Rowing upstream was easy compared to coming back. The country's pretty rough. We had to pick our way through rocks, dead-end canyons, ridges, and gullies. We're lucky we got here at all," answered Absalom. "I see you've got company. Who is it?"

"His name is Ezekiel Fisk. It was his family's boat."

"They all right?"

"I don't rightly know because we can't find any of them. They're downriver somewhere. We need to look for them. I guess we can start in the morning," answered Angus.

"Ma's almighty anxious about us getting back," said Ansel.

"It will have to wait. Your ma will understand once I

tell her what happened," said Angus.

Come morning, Angus and Ansel set out on horseback. They each took a side of the river and began searching. Around noontime, Ansel fired a shot. Angus crossed over and found Ansel kneeling over the body of a young lass. "It's his sister, Sulie Jo," said Angus as he dismounted.

They took her broken body, covered it with boulders, said a few words over her, and went on. About a mile downstream, they found Zeke's mother. They did the same for her. By this time, it was getting late.

"We best get back before it gets dark," said Angus.

They made their way back to camp. Zeke looked at them and knew they didn't have to tell him. That night, they could hear him crying.

Come daybreak, the men mounted up again. This time, Angus held out his hand for Zeke. He lifted him behind him, and they left camp. At Sulie Jo's grave, they let Zeke have time to say goodbye. Going on, they stopped at his ma's grave. He threw himself on top of the rocks and wailed. They gave Zeke time to say goodbye and went on.

Going on downstream, they noticed something out of place on the river's bank. As they got closer, they saw what it was and sped up. They could see a body, half in and half out of the water.

"Pa!" shouted Zeke as he leaped from behind Angus.

TRAGEDY ON THE RIVER

Angus and Ansel jumped into the water and dragged the man ashore. Putting his ear to the man's chest, Angus could hear a faint heartbeat.

"He's alive, but not by much. Get a fire going. We have to warm him up if he has a chance at all. Ansel, go back and fetch some whiskey and blankets. There's a barrel at the wreck site," ordered Angus.

Ansel hurried off. They put the man close to the fire without burning him.

Ansel returned in four hours. They wrapped the man in blankets and tried to get whiskey down him. It came right back up, along with some river water.

"Pour some more down him!" ordered Angus.

While doing this, the man sputtered, his eyes flickered open, and he gagged.

"Take it easy," said Angus, "you're all right."

The man weakly nodded and caught sight of Zeke.

"Pa!" cried Zeke as he hugged his pa.

"Zeke," he whispered, "where's your ma and sister?"

"Oh, Pa!" Zeke cried as he buried his face into his pa's shoulder.

His pa nodded and began to weep.

Ansel had brought some bacon with him. He cut a sapling, stripped the bark, wound the bacon around it, and cooked it over the fire.

"How long has it been since you ate anything?" asked Ansel.

"Near as I can recollect, it's been over a week. I could surely eat," the man answered.

"What's your name?"

"Rafe Fisk."

"We are the McDougals. You were going to go right by our trading post."

"Sutler at the fort told us about it. We were going to stop. No use now. I have nothing to trade with. I don't know what I'm going to do," he answered. "I see you found the hogs and the cow. Did you find any horses? We had a couple of saddle horses and a good plow horse."

"We haven't seen hide nor hair of them. They're probably miles away by now. We've got plenty of horses at the post. We'll talk about them later. Let's get your belly full and get you bedded down. We'll talk more in the morning," replied Angus.

The following morning, they started back. At each gravesite, they stopped so that Rafe and Zeke could say goodbye. It was an emotional time. Tears flew as they knew the goodbye was final.

On the way back to the camp and wreck site, Angus was quiet. He had a lot of thinking to do. When they arrived, Rafe saw that his sons had loaded the wagon. He was silent as he took in what they had done.

"Let's go home," urged Angus.

A week later, they pulled up to the post. Angus called Rafe aside and asked if they could talk.

"Rafe, everything in that wagon and the stock belong to you. If we hadn't found you, we would have claimed it. I have a proposition for you. Instead of going on, why don't you stay here? I can buy your supplies from you. Or you can partner with me. Would you be interested in running the post? My daughter, Anne, and her husband, Frank, never have liked doing it. You think on it," offered Angus.

Rafe didn't know what to say. He pulled Zeke aside. "What do you think? Do you want to stay with these people?"

"Pa, it seems to me there ain't much use going on. Our dream is gone now that Ma and Sulie Jo are dead. If we go on, all we'll think about is them and wishing they were here. Pa, I want to stay here."

Rafe looked at his son in a new light. It seemed like he had grown up overnight. Rafe was proud of him. The grin on Zeke's face was all he needed.

Going back to Angus, he said, "If you buy my stock and goods from me, I would be happy to try. I know nothing about running a trading post and would have much to learn. If it doesn't work, we go on from there. Thank

you for the offer."

They settled it with a handshake.

Later that night, as Angus lay in Kate's arms, she spoke. "You did a bonnie thing today. I'm proud of you, you old coot."

"I just did what the good Lord would have me do. Let's go to sleep. I'm plumb tuckered out," he murmured while kissing her goodnight and drifting off to sleep.

THE TURKEY SHOOT

The turkey's gobble was cut off sharply at the report of a rifle.

"Not again!" grumbled Little Angus as he retrieved the headless bird.

"Pa, the next time we have a shooting match, you're going to shoot left-handed and twenty yards further back than us!" said Ansel. "It isn't fair, us shooting against you!"

Angus chuckled and got up from his shooting stance. He stretched his aching back, grabbed his shooting bag, and joined his sons.

"You know you can't beat me in a shooting match. I've been winning since I was a wee lad. Shooting has always been easy for me. I was the meat hunter for the trapping parties," he answered.

"We know it, but we can't help but try," answered Abner.

"Boys, I can't help it if you couldn't hit a bull in the butt with your ma's skillet if you were standing right behind it," he teased.

The boys glared at him and headed for their homes.

Three days later, the brothers held a meeting.

"I'm thinking we need to teach Pa a lesson," offered Ansel.

THE TURKEY SHOOT

"What do you have in mind?" asked Atticus.

"Well, I plan to get Ma involved. It won't work if she won't help," he answered.

"Ansel, what are you up to?" asked Absalom.

Ansel laid out his plan. The boys began laughing and shaking their heads.

"Pa gets a whiff of this, and he'll skin all of us," laughed Little Angus.

"Who's going to tell him?"

"I'm not!"

"Me neither!"

"Who's going to talk to Ma?"

"I will. It's my idea," answered Ansel.

"Good luck with her. You are going to need it!"

The following morning, Ansel visited his ma. Angus had ridden out with Absalom to check on the horse herd. His pa was out of sight before he approached his mother.

"Ma, we need your help," he said while sitting at the table.

"What do you need?" she asked.

Ansel proceeded to tell her his plan. As he spoke, a grin broke out on her face. By the time he finished, she was about to burst. She was laughing so hard.

"Can we count on you?" asked Ansel.

"I wouldn't miss it for the world. It's about time the old

coot learned a thing or two. What do you want me to do?"

Ansel told her, and she got quiet for a couple of minutes.

"Let me ponder on it some. It's going to be almighty tricky getting it done. I'm not saying it's impossible. I'll see what I can do," Kate offered.

"Thank you, Ma," Ansel smiled. "Let me know what you come up with."

Two weeks later, they had another shooting match. Angus joined the boys, and the contest began.

"I feel lucky today," boasted Angus.

"You do? How about we make this interesting?" asked Ansel.

"What's on your mind?"

"How about a friendly little wager?"

"You know I'm against gambling, but I don't consider a sure thing as being gambling. How about the losers, which will be all of you, having to muck out the stables and barns for a month?" offered Angus.

"Gee, Pa, I don't know. Sounds like an easy bet."

"Easy! Why, you young pups! Let's add castrating calves to it!"

"Fair enough! Let's shoot!" the boys chimed in together.

The match started, and Angus couldn't hit a target if his life depended on it. He was missing everything by a

THE TURKEY SHOOT

couple of inches.

"What in tarnation is wrong with me?" he muttered as he missed another shot. The more he missed, the madder he got. Ansel won the overall match and watched as his pa grabbed his rifle and headed for the house.

The boys chuckled as they watched him go.

"It's going to be almighty hard on him mucking the stables and castrating calves," giggled Little Angus.

"Isn't it!"

"Serves him right!"

"We have to get his rifle from Ma as quick as we can," said Ansel. "I have to get the rifle sights lined up again."

"If you do it right, he'll never know."

"With Ma helping us, it should be easy," said Ansel.

"You better hope so, Lord, you better hope so!" said Abraham. "We better go home before Pa gets suspicious."

"Aye!" said the brothers.

"You lost a shooting match?" asked Kate while holding Angus in her arms that night.

"Aye, and I don't understand it. Maybe I need a new rifle," said Angus.

"Is losing to them so bad?" she asked.

"We had a little wager going."

"Angus, you gambled on it? You never gamble. What did you lose?" asked Kate.

"I have to muck out the barns and stables for a month. I also have to castrate the calves." Angus moaned.

"That ought to teach you not to gamble," she admonished.

"Aye. I've learned my lesson."

"Good. Now go to sleep!" Kate said while rolling over to sleep with a smile. She had a secret to keep. She was determined to keep it.

THE HERD

They rode into El Paso, not knowing what to expect. Reining before the Acme Saloon, they lit down and tied their horses to the hitching post.

"This is as good a place as any to start," said Absalom.

"Do you reckon we'll do any good?" asked Abner.

"Hard telling," came the answer. "We won't get anywhere if we don't try."

Absalom couldn't help but remember why they were there as they walked through the batwing doors.

Angus had sent for them. They had gone to the ranch house to see what he wanted.

"Boys," said Angus, "it's time we expand. You know our ranch plans, and that means cattle."

"What do you have in mind?" asked Abner.

"I am going to ask a lot of you," he said. "I want you to go to Texas and bring back a herd of longhorns."

Absalon and Abner were speechless. Texas was beyond their wildest dreams.

"Pa, are you sure?" asked Abner.

"As sure as I will ever be. You can buy longhorns for two or three dollars a head. I have the money set aside for it. You will have to hire a crew to get the cattle back here. You will also need a chuckwagon, a cook, and a remuda.

Do you think you can pull it off?" asked Angus.

"Pa," answered Absalom, "I think so, and we're willing to try. You had better do a heap of praying. We're going to need it."

"I'm aware of that," Angus answered. "I'm figuring a month to get to El Paso if everything goes all right, then two months to buy the cattle and three months to drive them back."

"That sounds about right," said Abner.

"Boys, the trip will be dangerous. There will be outlaws and rustlers, and you will be smack dab in the middle of Indian territory."

"We know what to do. You have pounded it into our heads since we were lads. Don't trust anybody. Ride the backcountry. Don't skyline yourself and travel at night," answered Absalom.

Angus looked at his sons with pride. He had taught them well. He figured that if any of his boys could do it, these two could.

"I want you to pull out the day after tomorrow. It gives you time to say your goodbyes and get ready."

"Yes, Pa," answered both of the brothers.

The family gathered the morning Absalom and Abner left.

"I wish I could go," complained Little Angus.

McDougal's Glen

One look from Angus told him he had better be quiet.

Angus bowed and prayed, "Father, watch over these boys and bring them home safe. Amen."

Absalom kissed Rebeccah, Abner kissed Rachel, and both kissed their ma. The brothers forded the river and rode away.

The women shed tears as the brothers disappeared into the horizon. Angus took Kate into his arms, and they slowly walked back to the ranch house.

"Angus," she said, "you had better pray they come home."

"I have been, Kate, I have been."

Now, Absalom and Abner were on their own. They kept to the backcountry and were able to avoid the Indians as taught.

One month to the day, the brothers rode into El Paso. Tired, dusty, and thirsty, they bellied up to the bar. The barkeeper brought them beers, and they relaxed.

"I never knew a beer could taste so good," sighed Abner.

"Sure does!"

Motioning for the bartender, they asked him a question.

"We are looking to buy some longhorns," said Absalom.

"Buy longhorns?" laughed the bartender. "Why buy them when you can get all you want down by the Rio

THE HERD

Grande? Hundreds of the most cantankerous critters you ever saw free for the taking."

"All we have to do is round them up?" asked Abner.

"That's right," laughed the bartender. "Good luck."

The boys found a mercantile and bought supplies. Riding out of town, they headed north along the river. Finding a place to camp, they settled in, cooked supper, and turned in.

"This should be easy," said Abner.

"We'll see," answered Absalom.

They started their search after breakfast. Abner spotted a couple of longhorns and took out after them. He cornered one, and it charged him. A thousand pounds of angry beef with an eight-foot span of needle-sharp horns came after him. He got away from it and reined in his horse.

"Absalom, how are we going to do it?" he asked.

They were interrupted by laughter coming from a nearby grove of trees.

"Whatcha gonna do if ya catch one?" came the shout.

The boys watched as a figure emerged from the trees. They could see that it was a man astride a horse. He reined in about twenty feet from them and stared.

"Whatcha doin' out here?" he asked.

"We're trying to catch some longhorns," answered Absalom.

"How many have you caught?"

"We haven't caught any yet."

"I can see that," chuckled the man.

"Who are you?" asked Abner.

"You can call me Slim."

"We're the McDougals. I'm Absalom, and this is my brother, Abner. We came down from Idaho territory looking for cattle to take home."

"Just the two of you?" asked Slim.

"We need to hire men to help us," answered Abner.

"How much are you paying?"

"How's thirty a month plus your vittles," answered Abner.

"Most hands around here get forty a month," said Slim.

"Sounds reasonable. We'll pay forty if we can get a herd gathered."

Slim nodded and said, "I'll be back." Then he rode away.

"What do you think? Think Pa would go along with it?" asked Abner.

"Pa isn't here."

Toward evening, they heard hoofprints and backed away from the fire. Angus had taught them that. The light of a fire played tricks on your eyes. In the darkness, you can focus better.

THE HERD

"Hello, the camp!"

"Who are you?" called Abner.

"Slim and a few friends."

"Come in slow so we can see you. Keep your hands away from your six-shooters," ordered Absalom.

Slim came into view with a smile on his face.

"I like a man who doesn't take any chances. Can we come in?" he asked.

Slim and five men came up to the fire and waited.

"I'd feel downright comfortable if you unbuckled your gun belts," said Absalom.

"Mister, that ain't happening. Down here, a man feels bare butt naked without his guns," answered Slim.

"Why did you come back?" asked Abner.

"You're looking for help, and we're looking for work. Jobs are few and far between down here, and money is hard to come by," answered Slim.

"How do we know you're not going to shoot us and take what we have?" asked Absalom.

"If we were going to do that, you'd already be dead," answered Slim.

Relieved, Absalom nodded to Abner, and they lowered their guns and relaxed.

"Coffee's in the pot. Help yourselves."

"Don't mind if we do," answered Slim.

"Want to go to Idaho territory?" asked Abner.

"Never been there, so why not?" answered Slim as he turned to the other men. "This is Bob, Jake, Shorty, Blake, and Newt. They are all good cowhands."

"What are you planning?" asked Shorty.

"Rounding up a herd of longhorns and taking them back. We're planning on having a ranch back home."

"Tell me about Idaho," asked Blake.

Absalom told the men about their valley. He told them about how they got there and their big plans.

"We're going to need more men. Have you given any thought to a remuda? Each man will need at least four horses. It is almighty hard on a horse to herd cattle," asked Slim.

"Have you thought about a chuckwagon and cook?" asked Bob. "A man has to have something good to eat."

"We know, and we prepared for it," answered Absalom.

"I might know some more men," offered Newt.

"Can we trust them?"

Newt nodded and spoke. "I may know a cook. Riley is a good one. It would be worth it if we can put up with him."

"I've eaten his cooking before. Right tolerable," added Jake.

"I'll talk to him," said Newt.

THE HERD

"There's a wagon for sale at the livery," said Shorty.

"You're hired," said Abner. "Tomorrow morning, we start."

Thus began the roughest work the boys had ever done. Rounding up critters that don't want to be caught was a nightmare. Word got out that they were hiring and buying horses, and their remuda of saddle horses grew. By the end of the second week, there was a crew of fifteen, a remuda of good horses, a chuckwagon, and a grumpy old cook.

By the end of the month, the crew had gathered over three hundred head of longhorns. It had been backbreaking and dangerous work.

"How many more do we need?" asked Abner.

"As many as we can get. We'll lose some along the way. We may have to eat a few," answered Absalom.

Word got out that they were doing a drive, and men began showing up with cattle for sale.

"How much are you paying?"

"Two dollars a head," answered Absalom.

"Gold?"

"That's right."

"Mister, I can't remember the last time I saw hard money. How many do you want?"

"All we can get," answered Absalom.

"We'll be back."

By the end of the second month, they had a large herd of longhorns ready to go back to Idaho.

"How many do you think we have?" asked Abner.

"Somewhere north of a thousand head," answered Absalom.

The morning they pulled out for home was a relief for the men. It had been exhausting work. The first couple of days on the trail were a nightmare. The cattle kept breaking away and tried to return to where they came from.

Slim pulled up beside Absalom and spoke. "It'll get easier. Once the herd is trail broke, they'll settle down."

From his saddlebag, Slim retrieved a bell. "See that old brindle bull leading the way? If we can get this bell around his neck, it'll quiet down the herd. When the herd hears it, they'll know everything's all right."

Getting the bell on the bull was a chore. The men had to drop him on his side, jump on him, cover his head with a blanket, and then get the bell around his neck. He wasn't happy and proved it when they turned him loose. He was mad and wanted to stomp whoever was in his path. After a while, the bull settled down and returned to lead the herd.

Nobody said the trip was going to be easy. That was proven when the cattle stampeded during a thunderstorm. It took two days to round them up again.

When they entered Indian country, the Indians wanted

THE HERD

twenty longhorn steers as payment to pass through their land.

"Absalom," said Slim, "if we don't, they'll stampede the herd. You'll lose more than what we have to pay them."

Absalom agreed, and they cut twenty longhorns from the herd.

"This is gonna be downright comical!" said Slim. "Indians have no idea how to herd cattle, let alone the meanest critters the good Lord ever created!"

All the men laughed as they watched the Indian's efforts to take the cattle away.

"They may bring them back to us," laughed Absalom.

One day, a rough-looking group of men stood in their way.

"We're taking the herd," sneered the leader.

Slim answered him with a bullet right between the eyes.

"Anybody else?" he challenged. "I'm willing to get the ball started if you are!"

The men backed off and went their way, which was good. The Texans knew how to fight and were good with their guns.

"That was close," said a relieved Abner.

"Maybe, maybe not," said Slim. "Take a look yonder at the chuckwagon."

McDougal's Glen

Abner looked and noticed the cook crouched down behind the wagon with a rifle in his hands.

"Cookie's got a Sharps. Ever see what one of them can do? It ain't pretty!"

Abner nodded and was thankful. These men were willing to fight for the McDougals.

After that, there were no more mishaps other than the usual: thrown horseshoes, sore and aching muscles, running out of supplies. Things that normally happen on a trail drive.

They did learn a hard lesson one day. Blake made a mistake and criticized Riley's cooking.

"Cookie," he said, "these biscuits are as hard as a rock."

Riley glared at Blake and threw the rest of the biscuits in the fire. That was the last biscuit they saw until they got home. He burned the bacon, charred the beefsteak, and ruined the beans.

"Blake, you better say you're sorry!" warned Slim. He tried, but it did no good. All of the men went hungry.

They were about ten miles from home when they spotted a single rider in the distance. As the rider got closer, they could see it was Angus. Riding ahead, Absalom and Abner met up with their pa.

"You're a sight for sore eyes!" shouted Angus.

"Pa, good to see you!" shouted Absalom.

THE HERD

They dismounted and hugged each other. Angus had tears in his eyes, and he wasn't afraid to let his tears show.

"How did you do?"

"Pa, we've got almost a thousand Longhorns. We rounded up some of them ourselves and had to buy the rest for two dollars a head," answered Absalom.

"You did good," praised Angus. "Did you have any trouble?"

"We'll talk later. Let's get these critters home," answered Absalom.

They got the cattle across the river, up the hill, and into the cave. The cattle weren't happy about the cave, but they pushed them out on the bench and into the glen.

Slim and the men reined in and sat in amazement.

"This is yours?"

"Yes, forty thousand acres, give or take a few," answered Abner.

"What a spread! It's downright beautiful!"

Angus rode up to them and spoke. "I want to thank you for what you did. I know you're a long way from home. Would any of you want to stay and work for us?"

"Same pay?" asked one of the cowboys.

"Yes, same pay. We have built a bunkhouse and corral down a ways into the glen. Ready for any of you who want to stay," offered Angus.

"Pa, Slim was a big help. He helped us find more men," said Abner.

"Slim, I'll make you foreman if you stay."

"I'm in. Be glad to work for you," answered Slim.

"Any more?" asked Angus.

Some of the men were homesick and started for home. Angus was able to hire seven and was glad to get them.

It was a happy homecoming. The women prepared a huge meal for everybody. There was laughter and singing. Angus and Kate were elated. They made the new men feel at home, and all was good.

That night, Kate rolled into Angus's arms and spoke. "They did it! They brought a herd here from Texas!"

"That they did. I put a lot of trust in them, and they came through. I'm downright proud of them," Angus happily said.

"I hear they didn't spend all the money," questioned Kate.

"No, they were wise with it. That tells me they can continue after you and I are gone," smiled Angus.

"I hear the cook is staying too. I also hear he is a grump," snickered Kate.

"I heard that too. Time will tell."

"You old coot! I love you and what we are doing. You did good!"

"Thank you, Kate."

"Good night."

"Good night."

THE RUNAWAY

Angus was up early. He usually was up at daybreak, but this was something different. For some reason, the patriarch had a feeling something was wrong. In the past, he had experienced the same thing and had always been right. Kate was still asleep. He quietly made a pot of coffee, poured a cupful, and eased himself out the door. The sun was just a sliver on the horizon, and a nip was in the air. He was glad he had put on his buckskin jacket. It felt almighty good.

The feeling wouldn't leave him, so he decided he had better take a look. He slowly walked around the ranch house and was satisfied nothing was wrong. He worked his way toward the barn. He was on the backside of it when he made a discovery. It had rained the day before, and in the mud, he found footprints. They were small, like something a child would make.

"Well, now, looky here," he thought. "I wonder who's young'un made these tracks."

He could see tracks going into the barn and coming out. Opening the barn door, Angus began his search. He found a place in the loft where someone had bedded down in the loose hay. An old, crumpled horse blanket was lying there, and he found a tin cup with remnants of milk in the bottom of it.

"Someone's sleeping up here and helping themselves to our milk. No wonder Bossie hasn't been giving us much lately. Somebody's beating us to it!"

He went back to the house. Kate was up, biscuits were in the Dutch oven, sitting on a bed of coals, and bacon was frying.

She saw the puzzled look on his face and spoke. "Something wrong? You look almighty confused!"

Angus told her, "I found some wee one's tracks by the barn, and someone's been sleeping in the loft. Someone has milked Bossie. I found a tin cup with drops of milk in the bottom of it."

"Any idea who it might be?"

"No, I have no clue. Don't suppose it's any of the lads or lassies, do you?"

"I would hardly think so. It's getting too cold at night to leave a warm bed and sleep in a drafty barn," Kate answered.

"That's what I was thinking, too. I'll talk to the boys. Maybe they know something."

After breakfast, Angus started asking around. None of the boys knew anything about it.

"No, Pa, all our lads and lasses were in bed last night," each had answered.

It was a mystery that had to be solved. Angus had to find out who it was and why they slept in the barn. He was also upset about the lost milk. Fresh milk was a rarity on the frontier. They couldn't afford to lose it. He and Kate talked about it later.

"I know it's a wee one. I'm wondering if it's in trouble."

"Most likely," answered Kate. "I'm sure it's hungry and probably scared. What are you going to do?"

"How about you fix me a plate of vittles? I'll go out there before dark and try to catch them. If you hear me yelp, come running," he replied.

Angus set the plate on top of a barrel by the loft ladder and found himself a good place to hide. The sun went down, it got quiet, and the temperature began to drop. He knew that if anything were going to happen, it would be soon. He had pulled his coat up around his ears when he heard it. The barn door creaked softly, and a dark form slowly crept toward the ladder. It stopped, picked up the plate, looked in all directions for danger, smelled it, and began stuffing vittles into its mouth as fast as it could. Angus got to his feet and was on the intruder before it knew he was there. Grabbing ahold of it, he shouted. "I got you!"

Whatever it was, it put up a good fight. It kicked, squirmed, and bit, trying to get away.

Angus let out a yelp, "Kate, I need you!"

THE RUNAWAY

A short time later, Kate came through the door carrying a lantern.

"Land sakes, Angus, you're hollering loud enough to wake everybody up!"

"You try to hold it!" he glared back at her.

"What have you got?"

"Once I get a better hold, we'll find out!"

Angus finally got control, and Kate held the lantern close. It was clear he had ahold of a boy. He was filthy. His clothes were rags. Physically, he was nothing but skin and bones. Every time Angus held him tight, he winced and whimpered in pain.

"Boy! I'm not going to hurt you! Now settle down and quit fighting me!"

That only made him struggle harder.

"I said settle down!"

"Let me try," said Kate. She set the lantern down and took a piece of hard candy from her shawl pocket.

The boy saw the candy and lunged for it. She was expecting it and kept the candy away from him.

"You can have it, but first, we need some answers. Who are you? Where did you come from? Why are you sleeping in our barn? Where are your ma and pa?"

He looked at Kate, the candy, and then Angus with tears in his eyes.

"Johnny Woolens."

"Well, Johnny, why are you here?" asked Angus.

"I can't go home. You can't make me!" the lad cried.

"What's wrong?" asked Kate.

"Not telling!"

Kate put her hand on his back. He winced and pulled away.

"Johnny, can I see your back?"

He looked at her, nodded, and lifted his shirt so she could see. His back was nothing but a mess of black and blue welts. Kate took one look and gasped.

"Come with me! We're going to the house!" she ordered.

While she was doctoring his back, Angus began asking questions.

"Who did this to you?"

"My new pa did it because he doesn't like me. My pap got stomped by a bull and died. Ma needed a man to take care of the place, and he came along. I could see what he was, and I didn't like it. From the day they got hitched until now, he has taken whatever he could get ahold of to my backside. I couldn't take it anymore. I up and skedaddled," Johnny answered.

"Where's your ma and pa now?" asked Angus.

"I don't rightly know. When I skedaddled, Ma and Jeb

THE RUNAWAY

were camping downriver."

"Any brothers and sisters?" asked Kate.

"Got a sister named Abbie. He likes her. He has a funny look on his face whenever he's around her. Sometimes I see him watching her. He scares me," trembled Johnny.

Angus started getting mad. It took a heap to make him that way. He could usually control it. But there were times when his anger raged inside. He could feel his rage building.

"Please don't make me go back!" Johnny begged.

"Don't you worry about that! You're going to stay with us. Kate, see if you can find something for him to wear. Oh, and fry some bacon. His backbone looks like it's rubbing his belly button."

A couple of days later, Angus was working in the barn. The door opened, and Rafe walked in.

"Angus, someone's at the trading post asking about a runaway boy," he said.

Angus stopped what he was doing and headed that way. He started seeing red as the rage began to build inside him.

In front of the trading post was a ramshackle wagon hitched to two run-down horses. A woman was sitting on the wagon seat, and a pretty little girl was behind her. Angus went through the door in a hurry. He walked up to the man and stared at him.

"Can I help you?"

"I'm lookin' for my boy. He ran off, and we can't find him," the man answered.

"What's your name?"

"Jeb Woolens. Why?"

Angus's right fist collided with Jeb's head, and he staggered backward. Angus waded in, punching hard and fast. Jeb went for his knife, and Angus shouted, "Pull it, and I'll kill you!"

Rafe had followed him onto the post and stood there, pointing a rifle at Jeb.

"I'm gonna lick you good and proper," snarled Angus, "beating that boy like you did!"

One thing Angus knew was how to fight, and many years on the frontier had honed his skills. Fighting meant win or die, but this was different. Even though Angus was twice Jeb's age, he gave Jeb the beating he deserved. After beating him to a pulp, Angus dragged him by the heels out the door. He took Jeb's knife, went to the wagon, and unloaded Jeb's guns. Angus saw the look on the woman's face.

"Ma'am, your boy is here. He told me what was going on. How he was beaten daily by that polecat of a husband you've got. There's no place for that out here. If you want to stay with us, you're welcome. He'll never bother you

THE RUNAWAY

again. Your little girl will be safe. You won't have to worry about him being around her."

She began crying and stepped down from the wagon. They gathered up her belongings and took them to the post.

"Thank you!" she cried. "I had no idea what Jeb was like when we got hitched. I couldn't stop him from beating Johnny. I tried to, but he told me to shut up. Said if I didn't, I'd catch it like Johnny. I was almighty frightful for Abbie. He was acting strange around her."

"It's over now. Let me take care of it," offered Angus.

Jeb woke up hanging upside down from a barn beam. His shirt ripped from his body. His arms were outstretched and tied off, pulling the skin across his shoulders taut. Angus was at his grindstone, sharpening his knife. Johnny was watching him.

"What are you going to do? Cut me down!" cried Jeb.

"I thought Johnny might have a little fun."

"You aren't going to cut me, are you?"

"Thought crossed my mind. It's up to him. Seems to me a little payback is due," answered Angus. "He might want to make your back look like his."

Angus got up from the whetstone and handed the knife to Johnny. He went behind Jeb and gently ran the blade across his back. Jeb began to cry.

"Please, don't," he sobbed. "I'm sorry for what I did

to you!"

Johnny took the blade and began carving "CHILD BEATER" across Jeb's back. Angus had to help him with the spelling. He was careful not to go too deep, just deep enough to leave a readable scar. Jeb screamed as his blood trickled down his back.

Johnny finished and handed the knife to Angus. Angus cut him down, glared at him, and spoke.

"By all rights, you should be dead. Johnny made his choice. Now, you have to live with it. If you ever come back this way, you'll die. The Indians are our friends. I'm going to tell them about you. They don't take kindly to child beaters. All they have to do is lift your shirt and see your scars. If you get past them, you have me to deal with."

"What about my woman?" Jeb asked.

"She's staying here. As far as she's concerned, you're dead. I suggest you skedaddle before I get my dander up again!"

Jeb hobbled out of the barn, got in his wagon, and checked his guns. He glared at Angus and drove off. He couldn't help but notice several armed men watching him. There were way too many for him to argue with.

That night, while lying in bed, Angus and Kate talked.

"Got your mad up, didn't you," scolded Kate.

"Reckon I did. There are some things a man can't let go

unanswered," he said. "Beating a boy and thinking about doing things to his sister is at the top of my list!"

"I heard you gave him a good whomping."

"This old he-coon can still give as good as he gets."

"What happened in the barn? He came out of there scared to death and favoring his back."

"Jeb was shown the error of his ways."

"Did you hurt him?"

"No, but Johnny had something for Jeb to remember him by."

"I don't reckon I want to know about it. I want to be able to sleep tonight," Kate sleepily replied.

Angus shut his eyes and prayed.

"Father, I ask that you forgive me. I let my anger get the best of me again. It's almighty hard to control it, especially considering what Jeb did. I ask that you deal with him. Show him that he needs You. I ask that you help me to be a better man. Amen."

Kate had listened to him. "I'm proud of you, you old coot! I would have been almighty upset if you hadn't done what you did. The good Lord understands what we have to do to survive. Be thankful. He's a forgiving God. Now, go to sleep. Good night. Love you."

"Love you too! You're a good woman," Angus said as he closed his eyes.

OBADIAH SKINKS

They heard it long before they got there. A gun went off, and a woman was screaming.

"Hold up!" Angus ordered. "We don't know what we're riding into."

It was spring, and Angus and the boys were looking for log jams downriver. There was trouble ahead, and they needed to check it out.

"Ansel, you go ahead and take a look. The rest of us will check our rifle loads, just in case."

Ansel did as ordered and came back in a hurry.

"Pa, there's a wagon up ahead. I saw a man and woman attacked by some rough-looking men. One of them was ripping a dress off the woman!"

"Hells Bells! We have to stop it! Let's go!"

Angus and the boys rounded a curve and were immediately at the scene. Taken by surprise, they caught the men off guard. Angus had them under his rifle sight before they could grab their weapons.

"Move, and you're dead!" Angus ordered.

One of the men got off the half-naked woman and turned to face him.

"You," he muttered while pulling his pants up.

"Obadiah Skinks! I should have killed you when I had

OBADIAH SKINKS

the chance!" Angus said through clenched teeth.

Obadiah glared at him. "What's stopping you!"

The feud between him and "Bad" Skinks began during his trapping days. He had hired onto a trapping party and had met Skinks there. Things began disappearing around the camp, and nobody could figure out why until they caught the culprit one day. Skinks had always admired Angus's knife. It was an original Bowie knife made by Rezin Bowie's blacksmith slave, and it was Angus's prize possession. He had put it in his pouch and had gone to fill his plate. When he got back, it was missing. He saw Obadiah slinking away and charged him. Angus sent him sprawling, and his knife flew out of Obadiah's hand. He grabbed it and turned to see Skinks coming for him, his knife in his hand.

Angus was ready for him. He was crouched down into a fighting stance. Other trappers immediately surrounded them. Taking a man's weapon was delivering a death sentence on the frontier.

"So you're the no-good skunk that's been stealing things!" shouted Angus.

Obadiah didn't answer him. He charged Angus, and the fight was on. Back and forth, they lunged. A slit here, a nick there, and the blood began to flow on both of them. Angus waited for an opening, and when it presented itself, he was ready. With a vicious swing, he cut most of Obadiah's ear off and cut a large gash across his cheek.

Obadiah screamed, grabbed his mangled ear, and stumbled away. Turning back, he moaned, "Angus, I'm gonna kill you if it's the last thing I ever do!"

Angus started for him, and the trappers stopped him. The leader of the party stepped in and spoke.

"Skinks, pack your gear and git! I've no truck with a thief. Return everything you have taken before you go. If I ever see you again, I'll kill you myself!"

As Skinks rode off, he turned and glared at Angus. "Watch yer backside because I'm coming for you!"

That was the last time Angus saw him until now. The rumors flew about Skinks. He heard Skinks had taken up with a whore and had a passel of young'uns. He also heard that wherever Skinks went, trouble always followed. Murder, rape, stealing, and burning were attributed to him and his family. Everybody forgot his first name. He was known as "Bad" Skinks. Now Angus was face to face with him.

"I've been hearing about you. I've also been hearing about what a worthless skunk you are. Raping a woman! Touching a woman on the frontier is the lowest thing you can do!"

He turned to the woman's man. Angus saw that the

man was almost dead from the gunshot.

"Abner, tend to his wound. The rest of you watch them, especially his daughter. Next to her pa, she's the worst of the bunch. She's good with a knife or gun and a bullwhip, so watch her. If she starts acting crazy, shoot her."

"Pa, are you sure?"

"Positive. She can knock a horse fly off a horse's ear with a whip at ten yards. Don't trust her!"

Turning back to Skinks, Angus looked him up and down.

"Bad, you aren't worth the effort, but you've got it coming," he said, pulling his knife. "If you win, you can leave. My boys won't stop you. You hear that, Ansel? Let him and his passel ride out of here if he kills me."

Ansel nodded and glanced at his brothers. They didn't like it, but they knew they would obey. They knew it would be a fight to the death. It was inevitable.

Angus looked at Bad and said, "You have always wanted my knife. If you can take it out of my dead hands, it's yours. I'm going to kill you and pray for your lost soul."

Bad looked at Angus and charged. Angus was expecting it. He sidestepped and tripped Bad, sending him sprawling in the dust. Bad jumped up and came for him again. Angus roared with rage, clinched, each man grabbing the other man's knife hand. Angus was an old he-coon, and his experience began to win out. He got his leg behind Bad's. By sheer strength, he tripped him, and down he went with Angus on top of him. Angus freed his knife, and the momentum allowed him to sink his blade into Bad's guts.

Bad screamed and gasped. Blood poured from his wound and covered Angus's hand. As Bad's lifeblood began seeping away, he began to tremble and cry.

"You killed me!"

"You're not dead yet. Are you ready to face eternity?"

"I'm scared!"

"I would be if I were facing Hell. You don't have to go there. All you have to do is repent and ask Jesus into your heart," Angus said.

Bad was sinking fast. Angus saw that he was mouthing words. Leaning close, he could hear Bad repenting of his sins. As he asked Jesus into his heart, a smile came over his face, and he was gone.

Angus rose and silently prayed, "Thank you, Father."

Angus turned to Bad's kin. "You're going to die for what you've done. It's the only fitting thing to do."

His kin erupted in cries and gasps.

"Please, Mister, don't do it. We're sorry."

"It's too late. The one you need to ask forgiveness from is Jesus. Your pa did, and now he's in Heaven. You can either join him or go to Hell. It's your choice."

Angus led them all to the Lord, except his daughter. He placed the noose around her neck. She cursed him and spat in his face. Angus swatted her horse's rump, and it ran out from under him. He watched her body convulse and then become still. Shaking his head, he turned away and rejoined his sons.

"Pa, it doesn't make sense. She chose to go to Hell instead of Heaven."

"Satan deceived her. It's sad, but it's true."

One of his sons asked, "Are we going to bury them?"

Angus answered, "It's the Christian thing to do, so yes, let's bury them."

That night, while lying in Kate's arms, they talked.

"Bad repented? I can't hardly believe it!"

"He did, by golly, he did. Kate, you should have seen the look on his face when he died. It was the biggest smile you ever saw."

"Do you think he saw Jesus?"

"I'm sure he did. Why else would he smile?"

"You old coot! You did well today! I'm proud of you!"

"Thank you, Kate. It means a lot. Good night."

"Good night. I love you!'

"I love you, too!"

CROWS!

Angus jumped up from the table and ran to the door. Something was wrong. The alarm bell was ringing, and that could only mean two things. School was starting, class was about to begin, or something drastic was coming. It could mean only one thing since it was the middle of summer. Trouble!

In the distance, he could see mounted men riding along the river toward the trading post. He knew they were soldiers by the way they were riding. They reined their horses in front of the trading post hitching post, and an officer dismounted.

"Morning, Angus," said the officer as he stepped up on the porch.

"Mornin' Lieutenant Wilcox. What brings you out this way?" he asked.

"Indian problems."

"That can't be right. Beaver Tail keeps his warriors in line. We haven't had a lick of trouble out of them."

"It isn't Beaver Tail's braves that's causing problems. There's a renegade band of Crows come down out of Montana. They're raiding, burning, and killing any settlers they find."

"Crows! I've had a run-in with them before! Some of

the best horse thieves I've ever seen! They'll steal anything they can get their hands on, including your hair!"

"We know they're in the area. They wiped out a small settlement southwest of here last week. We're looking for them," responded the lieutenant.

"We haven't seen hide nor hair of them. We'll keep our eyes peeled," answered Angus.

"That's why we're here. I need you. You know this territory like the back of your hand. I need a scout. Someone who thinks like an Indian. I don't know who else to ask," said the lieutenant.

Angus stood and studied for a couple of minutes. He knew there were enough men there to defend the place. That was no problem. If it got bad, they could hole up in the cave. They had plenty of food, ammo, and water. Taking care of the stock might be a problem, but there were always challenges on the frontier.

"I'll have to talk to my misses," said Angus.

"I wouldn't expect any less."

Angus nodded and went to the house. He could see her in the bedroom. Kate stood with her back to him, her arms crossed, praying.

"She knows," he thought, "but she always does. I don't know how she does it. She must have some sense when her man's planning on doing something she doesn't like."

McDougal's Glen

Bracing himself for it, he entered the room. "Kate. The cavalry's needing a scout. A band of Crows has come down from Montana territory. They're killing and burning out settlers. It won't be safe here if I don't help," he said.

"I can't believe you're the only scout around here, "Kate anxiously answered.

"I'm probably not. But I'm the only man who knows this territory better than anyone else. I'm sure I can find the heathens. Besides that, it's the Christian thing to do."

"You old coot! You always have to bring God into it, don't you?"

He knew he had won. He smiled and hugged his wife.

"All I ask is that you keep your hair. That mangy old scalp doesn't need to be waving on a Crow lodgepole."

"Kate, you know I'll be careful. I'm not afraid of the Crows."

"I don't know. You were almighty scared of my pa at our wedding," Kate teased.

Angus knew he had better go before she changed her mind. He grabbed his Sharps, ammo pouch, coat, and a pouch of jerky and went out the door.

"I'm going. Let me get my horse," Angus offered. "I need to tell my boys to watch out for trouble."

Lieutenant Wilcox nodded, and Angus went looking for the boys.

CROWS!

Mounting up, they headed downriver.

"Angus, have you got any ideas?" asked the lieutenant.

"I've been thinking about it. We need to talk to Beaver Tail. I'll go on ahead of you. He may not take too kindly to us riding in on him unaware. Indians are funny about that."

"Sounds good. You go on ahead. We'll be a few miles behind you. We'll stop and wait for your return. Maybe Beaver Tail can help us."

Angus rode into the village and found it in an uproar. A war dance was at a fever pitch, and the braves were mixing war paint. A cluster of braves were near Beaver Tail's teepee. Beaver Tail saw Angus and motioned for him to dismount.

"Beaver Tail, what's all this ruckus about?" asked Angus.

"Ahhhngus! We go to war!" shouted Beaver Tail.

"War? With who?"

"The Crows!"

"That's why I'm here. The soldiers are hunting them. They asked me to scout for them," answered Angus. "Why are you going to war?"

"Ahhhngus, my friend, the Crows attacked one of our hunting parties. They killed them, took their horses, and the game they had killed. When the hunting party didn't return, we went looking for them. One of the braves killed was my squaw's brother. They took his scalp. That is why we go to war. They will never come here again!" he cried.

Angus thought about it for a minute and then spoke.

"Beaver Tail, I have an idea about how to do it. What say we join forces?"

"No. Ahhhngus, white soldiers are too slow and don't fight like us. It would not work," said Beaver Tail.

"What if I go with the soldiers and we set up an ambush? You drive the Crows to us?" responded Angus.

Beaver Tail thought for a minute and spoke. "I will talk to the elders. I cannot make this decision by myself."

Angus nodded, and Beaver Tail and several warriors retreated to his teepee. He knew it would take a while. Each brave would talk, and a pipe would be smoked. Almost three hours went by before Beaver Tail came out and approached him.

"It is agreed. We will try this thing. Some of my braves say it is a bad thing. They think the soldiers will act like women and not fight. Ahhhngus, they must fight, or my people will think they are cowards. They would never help the white eyes again."

"I understand, and I'll take care of it," Angus replied.

"The hunting party was southwest toward the mountains. I will send scouts to find the Crows," said Beaver Tail.

CROWS!

"I'll go and tell the soldiers what is happening. When your scouts find them, we'll make our move."

Beaver Tail nodded and turned to his warriors.

Angus rode back to the soldier's camp and found Lieutenant Wilcox. He told him about the conversation with Beaver Tail.

"So, it's to be a joint effort. Good. When do we start?" asked the lieutenant.

We'll make our plans when their scouts get back and tell us where the Crows are. Lieutenant, your men have to fight. You don't want to make Beaver Tail's warriors think you're cowards. Hard telling what they'd do," said Angus.

"They'll fight! They'll fight or spend the rest of their enlistment in a cell! Will the Indians do what they are supposed to do?" he asked.

"Don't you worry none about that. Beaver Tail's mad. The Crows killed his brother-in-law, and he's out to avenge his death. You haven't seen a mad Indian before. It isn't a pretty sight. If they take hostages, don't interfere. They've got their way of doing things. If you try to stop them, they may turn on you. Just do as I say, and you'll be fine," Angus explained to the lieutenant.

In the morning, a brave rode into camp and talked to Angus. Angus found the lieutenant and told him what the brave had said.

"Beaver Tail's scouts found them. They're hiding in a canyon about forty miles from here. He wants us to meet him by the creek that runs by their village."

The three of them met and hatched a plan.

"We will send another hunting party out," said Beaver Tail. "We will try to lure them out of the canyon. If the Crows take the bait and chase our hunters, we will come behind them and drive them to you."

"Sounds good," answered Angus. "We'll sneak into the area and find a good ambush site. Send one of your warriors with us so he can tell you where we are."

Beaver Tail nodded and set the plan in motion.

Angus turned to the lieutenant. "We have to go. There's a lot of ground to cover before nightfall."

Angus, the soldiers, and a brave took off in a hurry. They bypassed the Crow camp and found a place they liked towards evening. It was the most logical escape route out of the area. A pass through the mountains lined with large boulders and trees. Angus motioned to the brave. They talked, and he left to find Beaver Tail.

"This is a good place," Angus told the lieutenant. "It's a perfect ambush site. Send half of your men over to the other side of the pass. And whatever you do, make sure nobody fires a shot until they hear one of us. We have to surprise the Crow. Tell them not to shoot any of Beaver

CROWS!

Tail's braves. That would be almighty bad. It's going to happen in the morning. No fires. We don't want to give our position away."

The lieutenant sent a sergeant with half the men to the other side. Before the troop left, he warned them as Angus told him to.

"If you make a mistake and reveal our position, I'll let you face Beaver Tail and his braves. Do I make myself clear?" he commanded.

They all nodded and left for the other side.

"We need to get some shuteye," offered Angus. "I figure we'll have our laps full of Crows long about daybreak. Whatever you do, tell your men not to shoot any of Beaver Tail's braves. I don't know if I could fix it."

The lieutenant nodded and passed the word among his men.

The sun had been up half an hour when Angus heard the sound of running horses.

"Get ready!" he whispered. "Remember, the first bunch is the hunting party. Whatever you do, don't shoot them!"

In moments, the hunters came into view with the Crows on their tails. Not far behind them was Beaver Tail and his braves.

"Wait for me!" he ordered.

Angus lined his sights on the Crow leading the pack,

took a deep breath, and pulled the trigger while he exhaled. The Crow toppled from his horse, and the trap was sprung. Gunfire erupted from both sides of the pass. Realizing what was happening, the remaining Crows swung their horses around to flee and were trapped. Beaver Tail screamed, and the warriors were on the Crows instantly.

"Hold your fire," shouted Angus. "You might hit Beaver Tail."

The soldiers watched with fascination as the Indians fought. Never before had they seen such savagery. It was kill or be killed. Beaver Tail's warriors won, and the battle was over almost as soon as it began. Beaver Tail rode up to Angus and Lieutenant Wilcox. He had a look of respect on his face.

"Soldiers fight good," he said.

"Did you lose any braves?" asked Angus.

"We lost four, and they will be honored tonight at our village," Beaver Tail answered.

"I see that you have some captives. What will happen to them?" asked the lieutenant.

Angus cringed at the question. He knew what was going to happen. He looked at Beaver Tail and nodded.

Beaver Tail spoke. "One will be allowed to go free. He will return to his people and tell them what happened. He will tell if they come back, they will die."

"And the others?" asked Wilcox.

"They will be given to the women. The squaws of the four dead will be waiting for them," answered Beaver Tail.

"Lieutenant, don't ask questions," said Angus. "There are some things you don't need to know, and this is one of them."

Lieutenant Wilcox looked at him with a quizzical look on his face.

"Remember where you are. The Indians have to protect their land the only way they know how. We better get home," explained Angus.

Two nights later, as he lay in Kate's arms, they talked about what happened.

"Glad you're home with your hair," she murmured.

"Me too! It's been right treacherous out there."

"Get things taken care of?"

"We sure enough did. The Crows will think twice before they come back."

"Good. I'm proud of you, you old coot!"

"Thank you, Kate."

"Good night."

"Good night."

RUSTLERS

"Pa, the cattle are gone!" shouted Absalom as he rode up to the ranch house.

"Where?" Angus shouted while rising from his rocker on the porch.

"The north range. Abner and I were checking on them. Found tracks heading off toward the Pine Canyon entrance."

"Sound the alarm!" Angus ordered.

Absalom raced off to the schoolhouse. Going inside, he began ringing the bell.

Angus stepped inside and called for Kate.

"Rustlers hit the north herd. I knew this day would come. I just hoped it wouldn't be this soon. We're going after the rustlers and cattle," he said, taking his rifle and pouch from above the front door.

"Angus, you be careful out there," admonished Kate. "You bring everybody back safe."

"Do the best I can," he said, kissing her and heading for the door.

He got saddled and rode to the school. There was a growing passel of men, all milling about and shouting at each other. Angus dismounted, climbed the school steps, and fired a shot into the air to get their attention.

"Quiet! We have to get the cattle back. We have no choice. Who wants to go?" he asked.

"Where's Ansel? Has anybody seen him?" questioned Angus as he looked around. As Angus talked, they could hear the horses in the distance. Ansel and his oldest boys came racing into the schoolyard.

Reining in their horses, Ansel shouted, "We've been hit! The horses are gone!"

"We lost the herd also. Blue Moon? Banshee?"

"Blue Moon's gone, as well as our best brood mares. They didn't get Banshee. He would have fought them," answered Ansel.

Blue Moon was the offspring of Banshee. Three years old, Blue Moon was a light grey color. Depending on the lighting, it made him look blue. A spectacular horse in every way. Except for Banshee, he was the fastest horse on the ranch. They had taken him to Fort Hall and raced him against all comers. He had won every race by several lengths.

"Well, that does it! Some low-life skunk watched him run and decided they wanted him. We'll see about that!" grumbled Angus. "Now, who wants to go?"

Everyone's hand shot into the air. Angus knew it would happen. He knew his family pretty well.

"I can't take all of you. Twenty of us should be plenty.

The rest need to stay and keep an eye on the ranch."

Angus heard the men grumble and had to quiet them down again.

"Ansel, Atticus, Abraham, I want you and your oldest boys to go. Frank, Jesse, do my daughters know you're here?"

"Yes, Angus, they do. Anne and Abigail insisted we come, and we want to go. This glen is our home. Nobody's going to take anything away from us. Whatever you need us to do, we're ready," answered Frank, Anne's husband. "Anne will help Rafe at the trading post while we're gone."

"Good! You and your boys are some of the best shots in the family. You've proved that whenever we have a shooting match. I can't say I've seen anybody shoot better than you."

"Thank you, Angus."

"Little Angus, I want you to come too. Be a good learning experience for you," he ordered. "Go home, get provisions, and meet me here in an hour."

They took off at a gallop, and the men were back in an hour as commanded. Angus noticed they all had coils of rope tied to their saddles.

"Good," he thought, "they're thinking ahead."

"Listen up," he ordered. "I figure the rustlers are heading for Fort Hall. Where else could they sell the herd?

What has me bumfuzzled is that the Fort knows our brand. They'd have to know something wasn't right. Let's find out."

Angus's suspicions were confirmed. They followed the trail through the Pine Canyon entrance, where it made a beeline for Fort Hall.

"One thing's for sure. You can't miss the trail. A blind man could follow this," shouted Ansel.

"Yup! Surely could!"

"Keep an eye out. We know they took the herds last night and are pushing them hard. We don't know how far ahead they are, and they're probably watching their back trail. I would if I was them," admonished Angus. "Everybody loaded and ready?"

They nodded or shouted yes.

"You lads, follow my lead. Don't do anything stupid and get yourselves shot or killed. Your mas and granny would be a mite upset. If you pull that trigger, always aim low," he added.

They followed that trail all morning, constantly watching the horizon for any sign. At about noon, they began finding stray cattle. One here, two there, standing spraddle-legged with their tongues hanging out. The cattle were exhausted.

"They're scared. We don't want to take the time to

round up strays. Little Angus, I want you to take a couple of boys and round them up as we go," directed Angus.

"Aw, Pa! Does that mean I'm going to miss all the fun?"

"Hush, boy, and do as I say," came the reply from Angus. "Gather them into that canyon up yonder."

Unhappy, Little Angus sulked and nodded yes.

After about an hour, the men noticed dust on the horizon. The dust hung over the scrub pines like a blanket.

"Ansel, you and Atticus come with me. Let's see what we're getting ourselves into," Angus shouted as he ran toward the dust.

Veering off, he began climbing a ridge. Once on top, he took a spyglass from his coat pocket. Looking ahead, Angus could see the herd in the distance. Satisfied, he motioned for the boys to follow him.

"Let's try to get ahead of the rustlers. We'll take a head count and then make our war plans."

The boys agreed. Staying just below the ridgeline, they managed to keep out of sight. Riding hard, they got ahead of the rustlers and found a good observation point.

"I count eight with the herd and four with the horses. What do you come up with?" asked Angus.

"I count the same, Pa," answered Ansel.

"I'll stay here. You go back for the others," ordered

Angus.

Angus followed the herd, staying out of sight and watching for a good ambush site. Ansel and Atticus returned with the rest of the family three hours later.

"What do we do?" asked Jesse, Abigail's husband.

"They will have to bed down soon. They've been up all night and have pushed the cattle hard all day. They will have to find water. That's when we'll make our play."

In the far distance, they could see the sun reflecting off the water. As expected, the rustlers drove the herd to it. They let the herd drink, and then they set up camp nearby. The rustlers hobbled their horses and got the cattle settled down. They started a fire, cooked their supper, and chose the night hawks to watch the herd.

"Real quiet like, we need to surround their camp. Take it slow and easy. Don't let the night hawks see you. We have to take them by surprise. Frank, Jesse, I want you to take care of the night hawks once the ruckus begins. Shoot them if you have to," ordered Angus.

Frank and Jesse started for the cattle. The rest followed Angus. Using hand signals, he divided the men and stalked the camp. As they got in place, they could hear the rustler's banter.

"This was too easy," joked one. "I guess we showed old man McDougal!"

"We can do it again. Any time we want," scoffed another.

"I'm going to make me a passel of money with that blue horse," bragged another. "Figuring on taking him to California."

"Think the soldier boys will buy the herd?"

"I don't see why not," added another, "once we take a running iron to the brand."

Sensing everybody was in position, Angus stepped out from behind a tree and shouted, "Hands up! We've got you covered!"

One of the rustlers went for his gun and opened the ball. Caught in a crossfire, five went down in a matter of seconds. They heard gunshots toward the herd and then the sounds of the herd stampeding.

"Drop your guns! Now!" Angus ordered.

The remaining rustlers complied. Lifting their hands into the air, they awaited their fate.

"Anybody hurt?" asked Angus.

"My boy, Andrew, got winged, just grazed. He's going to have a mighty sore arm," shouted Jesse.

"Too bad. Let's see to these polecats," retorted Angus.

Of the five still alive, two were seriously wounded.

"Patch them up for the ride back. Tie them up and set them by the fire. We'll turn in for the night. We'll round up

RUSTLERS

the herd tomorrow. They're dead tired and won't go far. Jesse, ride and tell Little Angus what we're doing. Take Andrew with you. Stay with Little Angus and the boys, and we'll fetch you on the way home."

Jesse nodded, and they left.

Come morning, they found the herd scattered for five miles along the creek. It took the men until midday to round up the cattle. Cooking a slab of bacon for lunch, they gathered around Angus and began asking questions.

"What are we going to do with them? Take them to the Fort?" asked one of the men.

"I've been pondering on it. Right now, with a dead tired herd, it would take us two days to get to the Fort if we all went there. First, we'd have to backtrack and gather up Little Angus and the strays. That will take a little time, and it doesn't make sense. Two or three of us could take the rustlers to the Fort while the rest of you started for home. From here, it would be a two-and-a-half day drive home because the herd is tired, and we can't push them. Cross country, it's a hard four-day ride from the Fort to home if we took the rustlers there. We've done it before. It's a hard ride. Or we can take care of the rustler problem ourselves. We'll have to explain why if we ride into Fort Hall with seven men draped across their saddles. It would be our word against theirs. Might not turn out too favorable for us," he answered. "What do you think we ought to do?"

"Well, we've always made our decisions by taking a vote," answered Ansel.

"Everyone would have to vote, including the boys. They're involved in this just like the grownups."

"Are we agreed?" asked Angus.

The men nodded, and they took a show of hands. After the vote, they loaded the dead rustlers on their horses, unceremoniously tied across their saddles. The five still alive were mounted, tied to their stirrups, with their hands tied behind their backs. Heading for home, they gathered up Little Angus and the others.

"Pa, I always miss out on all the excitement," griped Little Angus.

"Killing a man is serious business. Don't you forget it!"

"Yes, Pa."

It took them two-and-a-half days to get back to Pine Canyon. Stopping at the entrance, Angus turned to the rustlers.

"You know what the penalty for rustling and horse stealing is, don't you?"

"You're not going to hang us, are you?" cried one of the rustlers.

"If I don't, then every no-account rustler will think

we're easy pickings. Stealing a man's horse in this country is a death sentence."

"We won't do it again! We'll hightail it out of here!"

"I know you won't do it again. Boys, get your rope!"

Angus took a small Bible from his saddlebags as the men prepared the ropes. Opening it, he began to read to the rustlers.

"You must be born again to go to Heaven. You must repent of your sins. Ask forgiveness for what you've done. Any of you willing to do it?" asked Angus.

"Old man, you know where you can go. Unloose me, and I'll try to send you there," sneered a rustler.

"Boys! String them up!"

They hoisted all twelve rustlers and hung them high at the canyon's entrance.

The dead and those about to die hung as a warning sign to stay out of the glen. Angus found a scrap of paper and a pencil nub and wrote a sinister warning.

STAY OUT OF McDOUGAL'S GLEN!

OR YOU MAY BE THE NEXT ONE HANGING FOR ALL TO SEE!

He stuffed it into a rustler's shirt pocket, turned to his boys, and said, "Let's go home. That's enough killing for today. We did what we had to do. Don't ever forget it!"

"Angus," whispered Kate, "did you have to hang

them?"

"Kate, you know the answer as well as I do. There is no law here, no judges, marshals, or jails. We know the difference between right and wrong with the Holy Spirit prompting and always convicting us. It's the only way to survive here. Taking the law into our own hands is something we have to do. As long as we do it following what the Father teaches, we will be all right."

"I know," she whispered, "but it's a lot on your shoulders."

"Kate, I offered God's salvation to them. They threw it back in my face. At that moment, I had no choice. They chose Hell over Heaven."

"Why would anyone want to do that? It bumfuzzles me."

"Me too. On the way back, I prayed and asked for forgiveness for taking matters my way. I'm at peace with what happened. I'm all right," answered Angus.

"Good. Your conscience won't keep you awake tonight."

"Good night," he said while kissing her. "I love you."

"I love you too, you old coot! Good night."

SKELETON CANYON

"Pa, we've got problems!" shouted Ansel as he rode up to the ranch house.

"What kind of problems?" asked Angus as he arose from his front porch rocking chair.

"Something's killing cattle and eating them."

"Where?"

"The new canyon. It's not a bear or wolves. The strangest tracks Absalom, Abner, and I have ever seen. They're huge and almost human."

"Are you sure you're not imagining things?" asked Angus. "Sometimes your eyes play tricks on you."

"Come see for yourself. Maybe you can figure it out," answered Ansel.

"We'll ride out at first light. It's getting too late in the day to go now. No sense stumbling around in the dark."

"Me and the boys will be here in the morning. Any chance of getting any of Ma's biscuits?"

"Could be," Angus answered with a chuckle. "I'll see what she says."

"See you in the morning," said Ansel.

Angus nodded and went inside the ranch house. Finding Kate in the bedroom, he got her attention.

"We've got problems with one of the herds. We moved

it into a new canyon a couple of weeks ago, and now something's killing the cattle. The boys and I are going there tomorrow morning. Ansel says there's something mighty strange about it. He wants me to take a look, see."

"Be gone overnight?" asked Kate.

"Yes, it's almost a full day's ride from here. No way we can get it done in one day," replied Angus.

I'll have breakfast ready, so you don't have to go on an empty belly."

"Better make plenty. Ansel has a hankering for your biscuits."

"I figured as much. There'll be plenty," sighed Kate.

Bright and early, the boys showed up—Ansel, Absalom, and Abner, along with their oldest boys. Kate came out with a basket of sourdough biscuits. They emptied it in no time.

Chuckling to himself, Angus scolded, "You'd eat me out of house and home! Are you ready? If so, then mount up!"

"Tell Abraham he's in charge while we're gone," he told Kate while kissing her goodbye. "We'll be back in a few days."

"Be careful out there," admonished Kate. "You never know what you will find."

Angus nodded, and then they were gone. They only

stopped long enough to water their horses. Lunch was simple. It was Ma's biscuits. Long towards evening, they could see the canyon's entrance in the distance. Their longhorns were grazing out in the open in front of the opening. They also saw vultures soaring over the canyon.

"If my memory is right, isn't there a stream just inside the canyon's mouth?" asked Angus.

"You're right. It's not far inside it. A stream of good, sweet water. I figured we'd camp there tonight," answered Ansel.

"Sounds good."

They found a place to camp, hobbled their horses, built a fire, and cooked supper.

"I figure we'll investigate in the morning. It's too late to do anything now," offered Angus as he sat by the fire.

"I was thinking the same," said Ansel.

"This place is downright spooky," said Absalom as he looked over his shoulder. "I keep getting the feeling something's watching us."

"You noticed it too! I can almost feel eyes on my backside," shuddered Abner.

"Pa, it's so quiet here. No birds or critters are making any sounds at all. Wonder why?" asked Ben, Abner's son.

"I agree. I don't like it at all!" chimed in Abner.

"Are your rifles loaded? We can't be too careful out

here," asked Angus.

They nodded yes.

"We better turn in and get some shuteye," Angus suggested. "Tomorrow's going to be a busy day."

Along about midnight, their horses woke them up. They were raising a ruckus.

"What's spooked the horses? Listen to them! You'd think a mountain lion or a bear was after them!" shouted Angus as he threw off his blanket and stood up.

"I'd swear I heard something moving in the trees," answered Abner.

"Me too! When I opened my eyes, I'm pretty sure I saw something moving over yonder in those trees," offered Joe, Absalom's son.

"Now, let's not go off half-cocked. We don't know what's out there. If anything at all," Angus answered. "Abner, Ansel, check the horses. We've got you covered!"

The men checked the horses, talking gently and rubbing their muzzles to calm them down. Finding nothing wrong, they came back to the fire.

"I wonder what it was?" asked Absalom.

"I don't know. We probably better take turns watching the horses for the rest of the night." None of them slept well. They tossed, turned, and would peer off into the darkness, hoping to see something.

Morning came quickly, and as they were frying bacon, Ansel came running from where the hobbled horses were.

"Pa, come quick! You have to see this!" he shouted while trying to catch his breath.

Angus followed him to the horses. All around the horses, there were tracks, tracks like none they had ever seen before.

"Pa, they look like giant human footprints!"

"They surely do," he answered while studying the barefoot prints. "I've never seen the like."

"Look how deep they are. It would take something almighty heavy to make them," added Abner.

Angus stepped into one of the prints. It was half again as long as his, and Angus had a big foot.

"You reckon whatever this is has been killing the cattle?" asked Absalom.

"Could be. I don't rightly know for sure. Let's break camp and look for carcasses," ordered Angus.

As they neared the first carcass, the men weren't expecting what they found. It was a mostly eaten longhorn, with its head and neck twisted so that it was looking backward. The same footprints, plus many more, were all around the longhorn. They could see blood on its horns.

"Looks like it put up a fight. I can't think of a critter with the strength to break a longhorn's neck. I don't think a full-grown grizzly could do it. Let's find another," suggested Angus.

In total, there were six killed. The cattle all looked the same and had the same tracks around each one. The men made a unanimous decision. Move the herd!

"Come daybreak, we must roust them out of the canyon and head them toward home. We can't afford to lose any more cattle. Let's bed down here. Hopefully, it will be a bit safer," ordered Angus.

After another fitful night, all of them were up and ready to go.

"Watch your backside! I figure whatever it is, it lives in this canyon. Let's get this done before we rile them up worse than they already are," said Angus.

It wasn't easy. With longhorns, it is never easy. By noon, the men were pretty sure they had most of them. They had gathered them together out a ways from the canyon. True to form, the Longhorns didn't want to be there. They wanted back in the canyon.

"Let's head them for home," shouted Angus.

From the corner of his eye, Angus caught a glimpse of a large, hairy form watching from the tree line. He turned to face it, and it was gone. Angus stared long and hard but didn't see it again.

"Are my eyes playing tricks on me?" he muttered. "I

swear I saw something."

He couldn't get it out of his mind. What was it? Something that shouldn't have been there. Maybe Beaver Tail would know.

A couple of days after he got home, Angus went to see his Indian friend. Sitting beside a fire, Angus told him what happened.

"Sasquatch! You saw a Sasquatch!" Beaver Tail responded with wonder on his face.

"A what? What are you talking about?"

"The hairy men. That is what you saw."

"I've never heard of any hairy men!" said Angus.

"All the tribes know about the hairy men. They have been here for many years. Our forefathers passed the stories down from generation to generation. No one knows where they came from. We leave them alone, and they leave us alone," said Beaver Tail.

"Are they dangerous?" asked Angus.

"Only if you get too close. The hairy men will throw rocks and small trees at you. They will growl, roar, and scream to scare you away. They stink. You will know if one is near, and it will do whatever it can to scare you away," he answered.

"What do we do?" asked Angus. "They are in our valley."

"Leave them alone! Don't make them mad. I have seen one. It was two men tall and as big around as a buffalo. It broke your cattle's neck. What do you think it could do to you or your sons?"

"Nuff said," answered Angus. "They can have that canyon!"

"A wise choice, my friend, a wise choice."

McDougal's Glen

GOING FOR SUPPLIES

It was mid-July when Angus and his party arrived in St. Louis. Their trading post was in desperate need of supplies. There were sixteen wagons and twenty-four men and boys in the party. Every year, they took turns as far as who got to go. This year, Atticus, Absalom, Abner, and Little Angus, offspring, and hired hands had come.

They had always done their trading at Silas Wilkin's mercantile. He had always been fair with them, and they expected no less. As they neared the mercantile, a voice rang out.

"Angus McDougal! You old coot! How are you?"

Angus pulled the reins and looked around for the source of the voice.

"Farley Perkins! I haven't seen you in over thirty years!"

"Where have you been all of these years?"

"Farley, when I left off trapping, I set my sights on a valley in Idaho territory. I got a trading post on the Snake. Me and my boys came after supplies."

"Who are you going to for supplies?" asked Farley.

"Wilkins's place. I've always dealt with him," answered Angus.

"The reason I asked was, do you remember Jud Burley

and Seth Wookums?" asked Farley.

"I surely do. Bent many an elbow sipping from a jug with the pair before I found the good Lord," answered Angus.

"They bought Wilkins out. Ain't got no idea where they got the money to do it, but they own it all, lock, stock, and barrel," said Farley.

"Well, I'll be switched. Who'd a thought it? Those boys aren't smart enough to come out of the rain!"

"You know it, and I know it. Most folks around here think they are all right, but I got my wonderings," offered Farley.

"Why's that?" asked Angus.

"There are rumors afloat that folks that shop there don't live very long," offered Farley. "I know there's been a saddle sold three times. The same saddle."

"Are you saying what I think you're saying?"

"Put it this way. They've got a bunch of skunks working for them, that is, if you want to call it work. The laziest polecats I ever saw. The funny thing is, they'll supply a small party, and after the party leaves town, their hired hands disappear for a few days. Then they show up, and their mercantile is flush with goods."

"Mighty strong accusation you're making," said Angus.

"I know it. Angus, that saddle I was talking about. I put a mark on it when they weren't looking. That saddle has been in there three times. They sold it again yesterday," said Farley.

"Now that you mention it, I can believe it. I tried to share the good Lord. They laughed in my face," said Angus. "None of the trappers trusted them. Fixings started disappearing when they were around."

"Angus, what are you going to do?" asked Farley. "Is there anybody else you can trust?"

"Yes, Granger's place, but his prices are mighty high. I guess we had better go see the skunk's mercantile."

Turning to his men, he didn't waste time on particulars.

"Watch your back and pay attention. Don't go off by yourself. If you get in a fix, light off a round, and we'll come running."

Angus walked through the mercantile door and was immediately on the alert. The place was filthy; it stunk of sweat, urine, and grease. Several rough-looking men were there, lying on the floor. Others were drunk and passed out with their heads on the rough tables.

"Angus McDougal! What brings you here?" called Jud.

Angus looked up in time to see Jud and Seth come out of the back room.

"Jud! Seth! Farley Perkins told me you bought Wilkins

GOING FOR SUPPLIES

out."

"We did. It sure beats trapping," said Jud.

"I reckon it does," answered Angus. "I need supplies for my trading post on the Snake."

"I reckon we can help you. What are you after?" asked Seth.

"Got me a list here," answered Angus as he took it out of his pocket. "The usual plunder—tools, powder, lead, cloth, needles, pots and pans. We need flour, sugar, and coffee bad," answered Angus.

"We've got all of it," said Jud with a greedy look.

"Almost forgot. We need an anvil for our Smitty," added Angus.

"Got one," said Jud. "How are you going to pay for it?"

"We've got four wagons of prime beaver pelts. They aren't as plentiful as they were. We still get our share. I also have some gold with me," added Angus.

"Sounds mighty fine. Pull your wagons around back. Let me see your list. We'll start loading you," said Seth.

"Agreed," answered Angus.

Turning to his men, he spoke. "Keep a close eye on what we get. I don't trust them farther than I can throw a full-grown grizzly!"

Later that night, Angus and the men pulled out and camped a few miles out of town. The wagons were full, and the purchase was final. As usual, Little Angus was fussing.

"Pa, I wanted to check out St. Louis!" he whined.

"Boy, you're staying here. I'm expecting company," Angus ordered.

Long after dark, Angus and the guards heard horses coming. He alerted the men, grabbed his rifle, and waited.

Whomever it was stopped out of gun range, dismounted, and approached the camp. "Angus, it's me, Farley."

"Figured it was you. You make an awful ruckus when you're trying to be quiet."

"I never could slip up on anybody. Not as good as I used to be," answered Farley.

"Well?" asked Angus.

"Jud and Seth had a meeting with their hired hands. They were in the warehouse. I snuck up on it and listened through a crack in the wall. They plan on hitting you tomorrow night."

"Figured as much," said Angus. "Are there any of our old trapping buddies in town?"

"Come to think of it, I saw Squire Burns, Jacobi Gowans, and Wilson Berry in town the other day. There may be more," answered Farley.

"Reckon you can find them?" asked Angus.

"I reckon I can. The old coots won't stray far from a

bottle."

"Tell them Angus McDougal needs their help. See if they have any friends. Tell them about Jud and Seth and what they are doing."

"You planning what I think you're planning?" asked Farley.

"Now, what do you think?" answered Angus with a gleam in his eye. "I never could tolerate a thief or murderer, and I reckon they fit both."

"I'll be back come daylight," said Farley.

"I'll be watching for you."

Come daybreak, Farley rode into camp. With him was Squire Burns.

"Squire," greeted Angus.

"Angus, it's been a long time since we've seen each other. I have never forgotten when you shot that grizzly trying to chew off my leg. I'm beholding to you. What can I do to help?"

"Ride the ridge and watch our back trail. We're expecting trouble," answered Angus.

"Be glad to. I haven't been in a ruckus for a spell. Jacobi and Wilson are with me. I also rounded up Isaiah Porter, Zachariah Sumpter, Jim Burris, Tom Parks, Harley Coons, and Zeb Stringer. They heard you needed help and wanted to come," said Squire.

"Good men, all of them. Thank you kindly," said Angus.

"We'll be moseying along behind you."

"I don't figure they'll hit us until after dark tonight. Make sure of your targets," added Angus.

"Will do," said Squire as he and Farley rode off.

The rest of the day went by as expected. Late afternoon, they found a place to camp beside a creek. They circled the wagons with their back against a hill overlooking the creek.

"Gather up," ordered Angus. "Make sure your powder's dry and that you're loaded. I want four men up on the hill. The rest of you, except the guards, pick a place to bed down where you're a hard target to hit. Most important, we need a hostage. Try to wound one of the skunks."

The men did as told. At about midnight, the horses started acting skittish. Angus noticed it and whispered to Atticus, "Spread the word. They're coming."

From the darkness, a voice rang out.

"We've got you covered! Toss out your rifles and come out with your hands up! There are thirty of us. You ain't got a chance!"

Angus thought he recognized the voice.

"Jud? Is that you? You're going to have to come and take them from us!"

The answer was a volley of gunfire.

Angus and the men returned fire, which quickly got hot and heavy. He saw two of his party hit when it happened.

The raiders, caught in a crossfire, started dropping in their tracks.

Angus saw it and shouted, "C'mon boys, let's get them!"

They charged the raiders, and it became a free-for-all. Angus saw Jud and charged. They clinched and began thrusting back and forth with their knives.

"I'm gonna gut you like a catfish," snarled Jud.

"Many a man has tried. They all have met the Lord the hard way," answered Angus. "Come on, if you're so intent on dying!"

It was over in moments. Jud was a poor knife fighter. Angus broke free and, with one mighty swoop, laid open Jud's thigh. He screamed and fell to the ground with blood flowing down his leg.

By this time, it was over. The surviving riders stood by the fire. Out of thirty men, there were eleven left.

"Squire? Are you all right? Your men?" asked a concerned Angus.

"We're all right. Zeb had an earlobe shot off, and Jim took a round in his arm, nothing serious."

"Atticus?" called Angus.

Abner pointed toward the wagons. Atticus was clutching a still form in his arms. He was weeping.

Angus approached him. "Billy? Is it Billy?"

Atticus nodded through his tears. Billy was his oldest. He was a good lad, well-liked, and loved by all.

With a tear in his eye, Angus spoke. "We'll bury him on top of the hill. It's the only thing we can do. I'll read from the good book over him."

Atticus slowly nodded.

Angus went back to the fire.

"Your grandson?" asked Squire.

Angus nodded yes. Turning to the raiders, he stared at them with contempt.

"The raiders?" asked Farley. He already knew the answer. Their fate was up to Angus.

"I'll decide come morning," answered Angus.

"Squire, you and your men are welcome to spend the night. Not only that, I need you for witnesses."

After a fretful night, he made up his mind. Facing the raiders, he spoke. "Men, you're going to die for what you've done. If you want to meet your Maker on good terms, I'd be willing to oblige you."

"You're gonna hang us?" squealed a raider.

"Hanging's too good for you," he answered.

Taking his Bible from his pack, he read, "You must be

born again. That's what John three, verse seven says."

"Shut up, old man. I don't want to hear any of it!" shouted a raider. The rest of them agreed with him.

"So be it," said Angus. "Men, you know what to do."

The raiders were bound hand and foot, and the men tied a rope to their ankles and the other end to the saddle pommels.

"You're gonna drag us?" cried a raider.

"I'd hang you, but there aren't any trees," answered Angus. "All except Jud. The folks back in town will have something special for him."

They loaded Jud in a wagon and headed for town. Squire and his men took turns slapping the raider's horse's rumps while firing their rifles. The horses took off at a dead run, dragging their unfortunate captives to their deaths.

Angus and ten of his men pulled up in front of the mercantile. Farley dismounted and headed for the door.

"Wait up. Farley," shouted Angus.

The door cracked open, and Seth peered out.

"Seth, you get out here, or I'm coming in after you," Angus shouted.

Turning to his men, he told them to surround the store.

"Seth, I've got Jud in the wagon. He's still alive, but not for long. I'm figuring the town folks won't take too kindly to what you polecats have been doing!"

McDougal's Glen

From the back of the store came a ruckus. Atticus and Abner were dragging Seth behind them by the ankles. He had a broken nose and a swollen shut eye.

By this time, a crowd had gathered. Farley told them what was happening, and it quickly became an angry mob. The mob's intentions were obvious. There was going to be a hanging.

Angus spoke, and the mob quieted down. His reputation was well known in St. Louis.

"Before you string them up, I want you to tell me something. What happened to Silas Wilkins?" asked Angus.

Seth and Jud glared at him.

One of the mob spoke up. "We don't rightly know what happened to him. These polecats bought him out, and he left town. He said he was going to see his family in Kentucky. Silas was gone for a few days, and his horse returned to town without him. We sent out a search party and never found him."

"I think I know what happened," said Angus while turning to Jud and Seth. "You killed him, didn't you?"

The mob took charge and was taking him to a hanging tree when a gunshot stopped them.

"Before you string them up, we need to do something. They stole the mercantile from Silas. If he has family, it belongs to them. Jud probably has a deed. He needs to sign it over," said Angus.

Several men nodded in agreement. The deed was found and signed. Before Jud and Seth swung, Angus asked a question.

"Are you ready to meet God?" he asked.

"Go to Hell!" came the reply.

As Angus and the men left town, they rode by the bodies, swinging in the breeze.

Stopping by Billy's grave, they dismounted and gathered around it. Atticus had found a piece of wood for a grave marker. They piled stones high atop the gravesite and shed tears before saying goodbye. Atticus knew his wife would want to come on the next trip and grieve over their son's grave.

Mounting up, Angus wept as he thought about what had happened.

Then Angus lifted his head toward Heaven and prayed, "Father, I did my best. Forgive me for taking matters into my own hands, but it had to be. I ask that you watch over Billy until we see him again. Now, get us home safely. Kate's waiting for us. Amen."

FAMILY

The reuniting of the family was everything they all had hoped for. Angus and his family had highly anticipated the arrival of the McDougal and MacKinnon Clans.

Not long after Angus and his family arrived at the glen, Angus wrote a letter to their families that they had made it and everyone was all right. Angus had shared so much about the valley when he was home from trapping. Both families were intrigued and skeptical.

In the letter, Angus invited their families in Tennessee to the valley. He told them there was room for all of them. All they had to do was get there.

Angus forgot about the letter as time went by. Then, one day, a mountain man walked through the Trading Post door.

"Jack Dawkins! What brings you here?" he had asked.

"I was in St. Louis when I overheard the bartender in a tavern talking to someone. They were asking about you. He said they had a letter for you. I told them that I knew you and could get it to you. Here it is," he said as he handed the letter to Angus.

"Much obliged, Jack, much obliged," Angus had said.

Taking it to the cabin, he opened it before Kate,

"It's from my pa," he said. "They have sold their farms

and are on their way. Your parents are traveling with them."

"They're coming? They're really coming?" Kate cried.

"It looks that way. We haven't seen them in what? Six years?"

Now they were coming here. Their parents, siblings, cousins, nieces, and nephews. Eighty-seven people who were depending on Angus for their safety and sustenance.

The night they arrived was awkward and wonderful. There were family members they hadn't met, names that they had to learn, and who belonged to whom. The travelers were exhausted and turned in early.

The next day was a whirlwind of activity. Tables sat on the Trading Post lawn. A beef was roasting over a roaring fire, and the tables were full of food. The reunion had officially begun.

The families laughed, danced, and ate their fill. Kate's father, Robert, played the bagpipes, and Angus and Kate couldn't help but think about Scotland.

The Clan's patriarchs were seated under a canopy the boys had erected.

"Angus, you have told us so much about your valley. When do we get to see it?" asked his mother, Colleen.

"Tomorrow, I will show you our glen and where you will live out your days," he answered. "All I ask is that you wait until then. No sneaking off and spoiling it, please."

"We can't wait," offered Kathleen, Kate's mother. "But we will do as you ask."

After breakfast the next morning, he motioned for the Clans to follow him. Taking Kate by the hand, Angus led them up the hill and into the cave.

"We wintered here our first year," he told them.

Their families could see the Conestoga wagons lined up against the cave wall.

"Follow me," Angus smiled as he led the way.

As they followed him through the cave and out on the overlooking bench, he couldn't help but watch their reactions. They were speechless and stunned.

"All of this is yours?" whispered his father, Seamus.

"No, Pa, all of this is ours."

"I can't believe it! From forty acres of hills and ravines to this!" exclaimed Seamus.

"That is the same thought I had when I first walked through that cave entrance. There is only one word that gives it justice," replied Angus.

"What is it?"

"It is a bonnie, bonnie, sight," answered Angus.

"Aye, it is."

"I only have one more thing to say."

"What?"

"Welcome to McDougal's Glen!" said Angus with a

heart full of joy.

That night, as Angus and Kate lay in each other's arms, they couldn't help but think about what had happened earlier.

"The looks on their faces when they realized it was theirs. I thought I would have to hold Pa up!" chuckled Angus.

"I know. When Mother began to cry, it made me cry. But they were happy tears," sighed Kate.

"Have we done a good thing?"

"How can you ask that? We're finally all together. What we have done is a bonnie thing," Kate said while elbowing him in the ribs.

"Aye, a bonnie thing it is."

"Good night, you old coot. I love you."

"I love you too."

LITTLE ANGUS & SALLY MAY

"Angus, have you seen Little Angus?" asked Kate.

"Can't say that I have. Why?" Angus answered.

"He took out, on horseback, at sunrise this morning. Where do you reckon he went?"

"I've got a pretty good idea," he answered, while chuckling.

"Do you know something I don't?" Kate glared at him.

"Could be," teased Angus.

"Am I going to have to whomp it out of you?" she threatened.

Angus knew if he made her any madder, he would catch it. He was the head of the family only because she let him be. Angus knew this from past experiences.

"Now, don't go getting your dander up. I know where the lad was heading," smiled Angus.

"I'm waiting!" she shouted while grabbing a rolling pin and waving it.

"He's gone upriver to that new settlement I told you about."

"What for?" asked Kate.

"His brothers told me there's a girl he's sparking."

"How long have you known about it? Why in tarnation hasn't anybody told me about it?"

"I just found out about it this afternoon. Abner told me all about it."

"Well, I'll be! Do you know anything about it?"

"Not much. Abner said her name was Sally May Turnbull. They think she's seventeen years old," Angus answered Kate.

"Goodness! She's almost an old maid!"

"Times have changed since we went before the preacher. Remember the shivaree?"

Kate blushed. "How can I forget it? I was ready to take a skillet to my brother's noggins. Now, I do recall I was fourteen, and you were fifteen. Almighty young to be getting hitched."

"Twas, surely it was. But we made a go of it, and look at what it got us. Eleven healthy children, their spouses, and a passel of lads and lasses," beamed Angus.

Kate got quiet, and Angus knew she was thinking about the wee ones that had either been stillborn or died from a disease. If all had survived, there would have been sixteen children. Angus left her alone, and in a few minutes, she spoke.

"That we did, old man, that we did. But I got my wondering about Little Angus. Is he ready for a wife and bairns?"

"Time will tell, old woman, time will tell," he murmured while sitting back in his rocker and lighting his pipe.

The next day, Angus cornered Little Angus out by the barn.

"Well, boy, what do you have to say for yourself?"

"What do you mean, Pa?" he asked.

"You know what I mean. Out sparking somebody and not telling your ma and me. What's got into that thick head of yours?"

"Pa, I'm as old as my brothers and sisters were when they got hitched. I'm feeling I'd like to try it myself," he answered.

Angus stood and stared at him. The notion that his youngest was of marrying age hadn't crossed his mind.

"Well, boy, tell me about her," inquired Angus.

"Pa, she's wonderful. She's prettier than a June bug. She's got long red hair and always has a smile on her face. She likes me, likes me a lot. I really like her, Pa." he excitedly answered.

"Do you love her?" questioned his pa.

"I don't rightly know. I think I do. I can't do anything but think about Sally May."

As Angus listened, he thought about sparking Kate. He smiled as Little Angus told him.

"Pa, it hasn't been easy. She's got three brothers, and I've had to whip every one of them. It liked to wore me to a frazzle, but I got it done. They were almighty protective of her. Just like all of my brothers and I were for our sisters."

Angus chuckled as he remembered the brawls over his daughters. He figured turnabout was fair play.

"How long have you been sneaking out and seeing her?"

"Couple of months."

"Well, when do we get to meet her?"

"You want to?"

"Now, what do you think? Your ma and I would surely like to meet her and her family. Do you know anything about them?"

"They came here about six months ago. They came from Tennessee. Like us, they fell on hard times, packed up, and moved out here. Her pa's a blacksmith, and her ma's real nice. Cain't say much for her brothers," he said while rubbing his jaw in remembrance.

"Next time you see her, ask about us and them getting together. Like to meet them."

"Sure thing, Pa," he answered with a smile.

The families talked, and they set the get-together for a week later. Since it was the girl, the meeting was to be at her place. They all loaded into boats and struggled upstream against the current. Reaching the settlement, they pulled ashore and got out. Sally's brothers were there to meet them.

"Howdy! Welcome! Ma, Pa, and our sister are at the house. Follow us," said one of the brothers.

Little Angus and his brothers had a staring match with her brothers. They were sizing each other up.

Angus interrupted them, "Come on, no time for tomfoolery!"

At the house, they met her ma and pa. Sally May came out of a back room, and Little Angus introduced everyone.

"Ma, Pa, this is Sally May," he gushed.

"How do! Boy, she's a pretty one," smiled Angus.

Sally May blushed and smiled. "Thank you," she answered.

Kate looked her up and down. Satisfied, she nodded and smiled.

"Let's set a spell," said her pa. "Her ma's almost got the vittles ready."

"Oh, can I help?" asked Kate.

Her ma nodded yes, and the women headed for the kettles hanging over the fire. They had a lot of talking to do.

"Angus, we've taken a liking to your boy. Would be proud to have him in the family," offered her pa.

"Glad you feel that way. Today is the first time we've seen Sally May. We'd like to get to know her better."

"Why, surely I do. I don't blame you. I'd do the same if I were you."

"Let's eat!" came the call.

The food was good, and they sat around the fire enjoying themselves. It was a good feeling for both families. Getting toward dusk, they got up to leave. Angus called her pa aside to talk.

"We'd like to get to know her better. Don't suppose you'd let her return with us for a few days? I will guarantee her safety. Then we'll bring Sally May home."

Her pa stared at Angus for a little while and then spoke. "I'll have to talk to her mother," he said and went to find her.

They patiently waited until he returned.

"We reckon it's all right. If it's all right with you, we want one of Sally May's brothers to come."

"I was expecting it. We'd be glad to have Sally May's brother also."

Sally May kissed her ma goodbye and joined them in the boat. All the way downriver, she glanced at Little Angus and smiled. At the glen, Sally May and her brother, Josh, stayed at Ansel's cabin.

She came to the ranch house every day to visit Kate

and Angus. Little Angus was constantly by her side. He looked like a love-struck pup. It was plain to see he was smitten with her.

All too soon, the few days were over. They loaded the boats and took Sally May home. Angus and Kate were talking to her parents when it happened. Little Angus came running up to them, all out of breath.

"She said yes, Pa, she said yes!" he shouted.

"Well, I guess that settles it. We've got a wedding to plan," said her pa. Sally May's ma had a tear in her eye as she listened.

"I surely do believe so," answered Angus. "How soon do we want to do this?"

"Say a month from now. It gives us time to get ready. Sally May says you're a preacher. Is that right?"

"I am. If you're asking, I'd be proud to do it," answered Angus.

"We'd like that just fine."

"Then it's agreed. One month from today. Wedding at our place since they'll live there."

"We'll be there."

The month flew by in a blur of days. The brothers made a cabin ready for the newlyweds. The boys butchered a hog and a steer for the occasion.

"I now pronounce you man and wife. Son, you can kiss

your bride."

Little Angus gave her a big kiss, and the fun began. A lot of backslapping and elbow bending was going on. After the meal, the couple slyly disappeared. At least, they thought they got away.

"You planning what I think you're planning?" asked her pa.

"I reckon we are," smiled Angus while picking up a chunk of firewood and an empty wash tub.

"I haven't been to a shivaree in years. I can surely remember Ma's and mine. Liked to have scared her to death."

"Sounds like ours. What a ruckus Kate's brothers raised," answered Angus.

"Come on, time's wasting. I'm sure the brothers are waiting for us. It ought to be good!"

And so the two families were joined together. For better or worse, they became intertwined. Life on the frontier could be brutal. Little Angus and Sally May would either make it or die trying. It was what happened in the wilderness. It had always been that way and would continue to be that way. Families accepted it for what it was.

That night, Angus prayed while Kate was lying in his arms.

"Heavenly Father, I ask that you bless the uniting of

Little Angus and Sally May. Kate and I ask that you keep them safe and healthy. Tonight is a special time for them, so help them get used to each other. Amen."

He kissed Kate goodnight, rolled over, and shut his eyes.

Turning back, he spoke. "Lord, I forgot something. A bairn would be most appreciated. Amen."

Angus got a poke in the ribs.

"What was that for?"

"You know, you old coot!"

"Considering what is happening in a cabin not far from here. Are we going to let those two outshine us?" Angus whispered while reaching for Kate.

Kate rolled over, stared at Angus momentarily, smiled, and kicked off the blanket.

"I reckon I'm not over the hill yet," she whispered while rolling back into his arms.

"Well, praise the Lord!"

McDougal's Glen

THE POKER GAME

"Deal me in," said Little Angus, taking the last empty chair.

Outside, the wind was howling, pushing heavy snow against the trading post wall. The potbelly stove was working hard to keep the back room warm. The lid was off the pickle barrel, and a wooden platter was on a nearby table, piled high with crackers and cheese. There were no alcoholic beverages. It was Angus's rule and one not to be taken lightly.

It was poker night. The men played once a month on a Friday night. At least, they thought it was Friday. No one knew for sure. They just guessed at it. They kissed their wives goodbye and fought through the snowdrifts to the post. Their wives knew they wouldn't be home until sometime the following morning.

"Do you have any money?" asked Angus. "The last time we played, you couldn't cover your losses."

"Aw, Pa, I'm good for it," Little Angus answered while piling coins on the table.

"You had better be!" teased his brothers.

Little Angus took the last empty chair, and the game began. Angus was the first dealer, then Abraham, Abner, Little Angus, Atticus, Alexander, and Ansel.

THE POKER GAME

"What are we playing?" asked Abner.

"Five-card stud," announced Angus.

Groans could be heard from all around the table.

"You always win!" moaned Little Angus.

"Boy, if you don't like it, you don't have to play," returned Angus.

"Deal, let's get it over with," said Atticus.

"What are the table stakes?" asked Ansel.

"The same as always, a penny, dime, or two bits. Why? Too rich for you?"

"No, Pa, just deal the cards," returned Alexander.

The rules were the first two cards dealt face down. Then two dealt face up, the last card face down. The betting begins when the first card is dealt face up, with the best possible hand being four of a kind. Four aces and a king being an unbeatable hand.

Angus dealt the cards. The up cards were a nine to Abraham, four to Abner, a king to Little Angus, a ten to Atticus, a three to Alexander, a deuce to Ansel, and an ace to Angus.

"Not again!" moaned Abner. "Pa, you live with those aces!"

Angus cackled and tossed two bits onto the center of the table. The brothers glanced at their face-down cards.

Abraham, Ansel, Alexander, Absalom, and Atticus

folded. Abner and Little Angus matched the bet. Angus dealt another round. Abner drew a three, Little Angus paired up with a king, and the dealer got a jack.

"Your bet, boy," said Angus while studying Little Angus.

Little Angus peeked at his down card again, smiled, and tossed a dollar into the pile.

"Too rich for my blood," muttered Abner, throwing in his cards.

Angus peeked at his down cards and then stared at Little Angus. He matched the bet and bumped it a dollar.

Little Angus began to sweat. He again glanced at his cards and matched the bet.

"Pa, I think you're bluffing," he taunted.

Angus dealt the fifth card down.

"It's still your bet. You have a pair showing," said Angus.

Little Angus glanced at his down card. He never could keep a poker face, and this was no exception. He shoved everything he had into the center of the table, all eight dollars.

Angus studied his cards, stared at his son, and matched the bet.

"Call you. What have you got?" asked Angus with excitement in his voice.

THE POKER GAME

Little Angus turned his cards over and showed three kings. He began reaching for the pot, and his pa stopped him.

"Hold on, boy!" he said while turning his cards to show three aces.

Little Angus slumped back into his chair with disbelief on his face. His brothers began howling with laughter. His face turned beet red, and he got up to leave.

"I'm busted! The best hand I've had in a long time, and Pa beat me!"

"Boy, you can't go home in this storm. It's too dangerous out there. I can loan you some money. You can keep playing if you want to," offered Angus.

"Thanks, Pa," he said while sitting back down.

"Now, you're not getting off that easy. Get some cups and pour us some coffee. The pot is on the stove. You're going to work off the loan. You can watch us play if you don't want to do that."

"Aw, Pa, I accept," he said while getting the coffee pot.

"Abraham, it's your deal."

And so the night went. Back and forth, the luck ran. And, as usual, Angus was the big winner. One by one, he cleaned his sons out. And again, Little Angus was the first to bow out, then Atticus, Abner, Ansel, Abraham, and Alexander. They were getting ready to blow out the lanterns and candles when they heard pounding on the door.

"What in tarnation?" muttered Angus as he went to the door.

Opening it, he came face to face with a nearly frozen man. The man collapsed into his arms as a gust of wind shoved him forward. Abraham slammed the door and helped Angus drag the man to the stove.

"He's pert near frozen to death," said Angus. "Let's see if we can get some coffee down him. Abner, fetch me a blanket off the shelf yonder."

They wrapped him in the blanket and propped him up by the stove. He had no heavy coat or hat. On his hands were thin leather gloves. He wore a suit of black broadcloth and had on a blue ruffled shirt. He would have frozen to death if he had been outside much longer.

He began to shiver uncontrollably, and his eyes flickered open. He tried to sit up, but Angus stopped him.

"Hold on there. Lay back and take it easy. You're safe now."

The man nodded, closed his eyes, and went to sleep.

"Who do you reckon he is?" asked Little Angus.

"I don't rightly reckon I know. But I know what the man is," Angus answered.

"You do?"

"I'm figuring he's a professional gambler."

THE POKER GAME

"Are you sure?"

"I think so. Look at his clothing. Expensive and well-made. Peel off those gloves."

Atticus did so, and they inspected his hands. His fingers were long and supple, with no callouses or other signs of manual labor.

"Check his pockets."

In one coat pocket, they found a well-worn deck of cards. In another, they found three thousand dollars in greenbacks and a pouch of gold coins.

"Well, I guess that proves it," said Little Angus, nodding.

"Makes no difference. We have to help. It's the Christian thing to do," reminded Angus.

They got him bedded down and turned in for the night. Angus got up to check on him a couple of times. Satisfied, he went back to sleep.

Come morning, Angus got the coffee pot going and fried some bacon on the stove. The aroma woke the boys, and they bellied up to the fire. They filled their cups and piled rashers of bacon on their plates.

"Got any more coffee?" came a shaky voice behind them.

"You're awake," said Angus while pouring another cup.

McDougal's Glen

"I think I am," answered the stranger.

Angus knelt beside the stranger and helped him drink.

"What's your name? What are you doing way out here?" asked Angus.

"Name's Travis Burke. I was at Fort Hall. The sutler ran me off. I was winning too much from the soldier boys. They didn't have any money left to buy his high-priced goods. I heard there was a settlement upriver and had no choice. I had to run, or his hired hands would guarantee I never dealt another hand. They said they would break my fingers like twigs. I lit a shuck. My horse slipped on the ice, broke its leg, and I had to shoot it. I've been following the river, looking for a place to ride out this snowstorm. I saw your light and smelled wood smoke. I'm mighty grateful you opened the door," he answered in one breath.

Angus listened to him and turned away to think. He had no sympathy for a professional gambler. From past experiences, he knew them to be liars and cheats. That is, most of them. He had met an honest one once. He was the one who taught him how to play. The Friday night games with his boys were friendly, and he intended to keep it that way.

"Well, Burke, you are at our Trading Post. Angus McDougal's my name, and these men are my sons."

Burke nodded his hello and waited.

THE POKER GAME

"I'm a Christian, and I don't condone your profession. I also know I can't put you out in this storm because you're not dressed for it. I don't want a guilty conscience that I put you out and you froze. No siree, I surely can't. You can't stay here, and I can't take you home. My misses, Kate, can't tolerate gamblers. She'd skin me alive if I took you in."

"Pa, Sally May and I can put him up for a few days," offered Little Angus. "The bairn isn't due for a couple of months."

"Are you sure?"

"We don't have any lads or lasses like the rest of you. It'd be almighty quiet at my place," he answered.

Angus stared at his boy. He could sense something was going on and couldn't figure it out.

"Well, it's agreeable if it's all right with Burke."

Burke nodded, and they moved him into Little Angus's cabin. Sally May just about had a fit until Little Angus told her what he was planning. That afternoon, he and Burke talked.

"What were you doing at the Trading Post during a blizzard?" asked Burke.

"Once a month, we have a poker night. We get together for a friendly game," answered Little Angus.

"Don't suppose I could sit in? You say it's a friendly

McDougal's Glen

game?" inquired Burke.

"Pa wouldn't allow it. He doesn't trust gamblers. At the end of the night, everybody gets their money back. It's more for bragging rights than anything else. Pa hates to lose."

"That's too bad. I would have enjoyed it," Burke smiled.

"There is something you can do for me," said Little Angus.

"What's that?" asked Burke.

"Pa cleans us out every time we play. Either he's almighty lucky, or he's cheating us somehow," stated Little Angus.

"What can I do?" Burke asked.

"Teach me the tricks of the trade," Little Angus replied.

"So, you want to learn how to play poker," Burke replied.

"I surely do. I want to beat Pa at his own game," Little Angus said with determination.

Burke smiled, nodded, and spoke. "There's a deck in my coat pocket. I'll show you what I know."

Little Angus was a quick learner. Birke taught him how to read a tell on opponent's faces. He taught him how and when to bluff and how to beat the odds. Most of all, he helped him with his poker face and his tell. The month

THE POKER GAME

went by, and it was poker night.

"I'd like to come and watch it. See if you've learned anything," Burke asked Little Angus.

"I'll have to ask Pa. See what he says."

It was agreeable with Angus and the boys. The only stipulation was that he could only watch. Angus and the boys took their seats at the table, and as always, Angus dealt the cards.

"Five-card stud. Any objections?" their pa asked.

His sons moaned and groaned.

Little Angus caught Burke's eye and slightly nodded.

Angus dealt the cards and won the first two hands.

"Pa, next hand, let me cut the cards," said Little Angus.

Angus gave him a dirty look and shoved the cards his way. He cut the cards, and as if it was magic, his luck changed. Little Angus began winning. Little Angus won one out of three pots. By the end of the evening, it was between Little Angus and his pa.

Angus dealt, and Little Angus's up cards were a queen and a nine. Angus's cards were a king and a four. The pot was large, with almost ten dollars in it. Little Angus's last card was a deuce, and Angus's was another four. Angus was high with a pair of fours. He studied Little Angus's cards and smiled.

"I think you're bluffing," his pa smiled. "Raise you

another ten dollars."

Little Angus had been watching his pa closely. When his father got a good hand, he would scratch his nose. This time, he didn't touch his nose. Little Angus knew his pa was trying to buy the pot.

"I guess we'll see," Little Angus answered. "I'll match your raise and bump you five."

Sweat broke out on Angus's face. He peeked at his cards, scowled, and threw in his hand.

Little Angus's brothers started laughing. Abner grabbed his pa's cards and turned them over. There was a pair of fours.

"Whatcha got?" Abner asked his brother.

"A little old queen of spades," beamed Little Angus.

"You were bluffing me?"

"Yes, Pa, I surely was."

"Well, I'll be hornswoggled!" said a stunned Angus.

Little Angus smiled, his eyes twinkling, and nodded to Burke.

Angus saw the exchange and realized what had happened.

"I reckon you'll be moving on pretty soon, won't you, Burke?" probed Angus.

"In due time, Angus, in due time."

THE BLIZZARD

Angus had a worried look on his face. There was a definite weather change coming. He could feel it in his bones. That achy, nagging feeling you get when the barometer starts dropping. Now, he was on his front porch watching the western sky. It was a leaden gray hue, and a sharp wind had picked up, making him pull his hat down tight around his ears. Turning, he went inside the ranch house.

"What's wrong?" asked Kate. She was sitting in her rocking chair by the fire.

"We've got weather coming. Is the wood box full?"

"I filled it this morning," she replied. "We've got plenty stacked against the house. We should be fine as long as it doesn't get too bad out there."

"I better go check the livestock," he replied as he went out the door. "I'll be back as soon as I can."

"I'll have supper on the table," she offered. "I'll have some coffee brewing. It will warm you up."

Facing into the wind, Angus headed for the barn and corrals. There, his suspicions were confirmed. The cattle were lying down with their tails to the wind, and the horses were under the lean-to.

"What can I do to make things easier?" he thought

while tossing hay to the cattle and horses. "The water will freeze up. I'll have to get them some fresh in the morning."

Thinking about it, he got a rope and stretched it from the barn to the house. He had heard of more than one person getting lost in a whiteout and freezing to death within sight of their cabin or barn. At least the rope was there to help you find the way. When the storm hit, he had just finished tying the rope to the barn door post. A wind from out of the northwest nearly knocked him down. The wind took his hat and sent it sailing. He started to go after it and stopped, no sense taking any chances. It was blowing so hard he could barely stand up.

"I have to get back!" he muttered while grasping the rope and pulling himself toward the house. Reaching the porch, he stumbled up the steps. When he opened the door, the wind tore it from his grasp and slammed it against the wall. It took all of his effort to shut the door.

"Are you all right?" asked Kate while picking up things the wind had blown to the floor.

"Yes, I'm all right. It has the makings of a blizzard if I ever saw one. I got caught in one back in '22. We were lucky. We were using a cave and had some protection. We heard about another trapping party that froze to death. I knew several of them. It was bad. That blizzard lasted for five days. Who knows how long this one will last," he answered while removing his coat. "And I lost my favorite hat. The wind took it right off my head." "Supper's on the table," offered Kate. "Come and sit. You had better pray extra hard tonight."

Angus nodded and sat down to supper.

"Heavenly Father, we ask that You protect us during this storm. Watch over our families. I pray that they are ready for it. We ask that the blizzard will be over quickly. Now we thank You for this food. Amen."

That night, they lay in bed and listened to the wind howl. Angus got up and added wood to the fire a couple of times. The first time, he could hear sleet pelting the door. The second time, he cracked the door and regretted it. Again, the wind took the door from his hands and slammed it against the wall. The wind was pushing a lot of snow and had almost blown the fire out before Angus could get the door closed and latched. A fine dusting of snow covered everything.

"It's going to be a bad one," he told Kate as he crawled back in bed, "a real bad one."

The ranch house sounded like the wind would blow it down around their ears. The wind shrieked through the eaves like a thousand banshees screaming their lungs out. Angus watched the cedar shake roof overhead, and thankfully, so far, it was holding.

THE BLIZZARD

"Try to get some sleep. Not much we can do tonight," Angus told Kate.

After a fitful night, they awakened to the sounds of the storm's fury. It was the same as when they went to bed. Getting up, they got dressed and went to the front door. The house creaked and moaned under the wind's pressure.

"I'll get us something to eat," said Kate. "Can you get some wood? Better bring in plenty."

Angus donned his coat and gloves and found another hat. Opening the door, he was astonished at what he saw. It was a mess. Snow was coming down hard, so hard you could barely see because of the wind driving it. He stepped off the porch and sank mid-calf into the snow. Struggling, he rounded the corner to the woodpile. Grabbing an armload, he worked his way back into the cabin. He repeated this process five times until he was exhausted and frozen.

"It must be twenty below out there!" he moaned while warming up before the fire. "I have to check the livestock. If I don't get them some hay and water, they won't survive."

"Angus, you can't go back out there. It's too dangerous!" worried Kate.

"I have no choice. I tied a rope between the house and the barn. As long as I don't let loose of it, I'll be fine," he answered, pulling his coat back on.

Carefully opening the door, he went out on the porch.

McDougal's Glen

The rope was still there, and he grabbed it. Closing his eyes because of the bitter wind, he slowly felt his way. It took him forever to get to the barn. Shoving snow aside, he got the door open and went inside. Snow had sifted through the cracks and stood in drifts across the floor. Going to the other side of the barn, he unlatched the door that led to the corrals. Taking a pitchfork, he began carrying hay to the stock, which proved difficult as the wind kept blowing the fodder off his fork. Giving up, he carried armloads to the animals. Satisfied, Angus grabbed his axe.

"I have to break the ice in the creek!" he thought while entering the horse corral. The creek ran through both of them. All he had to do was find it under the ice. Guessing its location, he shoved the snow aside and swung the axe. In a few minutes, he heard the satisfying sounds of ice breaking. One more swing, and he was through. Going to the other corral, he repeated the process. Exhausted, he went back to the barn and sat down.

"I'm getting too old for this," he muttered, wiping sweat from his brow. "Better get back to Kate while I can."

He found the rope and made his way back. Brushing the snow from his hat and coat, he went in. He warmed himself as Kate stuck a steaming hot cup of coffee into his hands.

"Everything all right?" she asked.

THE BLIZZARD

"Stock's fine. They've been watered and fed," he answered.

"Good! Now set your old bones down," she ordered. "Here's your pipe."

"Thank you kindly, old woman," he said with a smile as he swatted her rump.

Evading him, she smiled, shook her head, and returned to what she was doing.

The blizzard raged on for three more days. They had gotten used to the wind and knew when it was over. Angus cracked the front door and faced a solid wall of snow. Leaning against it, it crumbled, and a blue sky greeted them. Looking off in the distance, they could see smoke rising from their children's chimneys.

"Reckon they're all right?" asked Kate.

"I guess we'll find out soon enough," answered Angus.

That afternoon, the family started checking on them. Travel was treacherous, but it didn't stop them. Ansel was the last to come. As they came in, Angus noticed they were short a child.

"Little Asa! Where is he?" asked Angus.

Ansel and his wife began to cry.

"What's wrong? What happened?" asked a concerned Kate.

"Asa was in the privy when it hit. The snow hit us

McDougal's Glen

before it hit you. We had a whiteout almost immediately. He got lost coming back to the cabin. I found his body this morning," sobbed Ansel.

"Didn't you look for him?" asked Angus.

"I tried. It was so bad out there I almost got lost myself. Instead of heading for the cabin, Asa went in the opposite direction. In the whiteout and the cold, it was impossible to find him. I knew he wouldn't last for very long out there. It's a horrible feeling. Knowing you have a child lying out there in the cold and can't do anything about it. It tears you up inside. Priscilla and I have cried until there aren't any tears left."

Angus and Kate gasped, embraced them, and wept with them.

"We'll bury him the day after tomorrow. Up on the knoll would be a good place. We'll have to build a fire to thaw the ground first. I'll take care of it," offered Angus.

The first death in the glen was the least expected and took a toll on the McDougal clan.

"And now, Lord, we say goodbye to little Asa. We know that he is with You. Take care of him for us. One day, we will see him again. Help us with his loss. In Jesus's name. Amen," prayed Angus over the gravesite.

The knoll became the family graveyard. It became the final resting place for more of the family.

It is always the hardest with the first. But the McDougals were strong and would survive.

GOING SWIMMING

It was hot! Too dadgum hot to do anything. Any critter on the ranch with brains was either lying under a shade tree or was knee deep in the stream. The hay needed cutting, the firewood needed splitting, and the garden needed weeding. All of this still needed to be done. Sweat dripped off the end of your nose while standing perfectly still. Doing anything physical was out of the question.

Angus rose from his rocking chair, saddled his horse, and rode to church. Going inside, he began ringing the bell. In no time, the churchyard was full of family and hired hands.

"What's wrong?" asked Ansel.

"Why did you ring the bell?" asked Atticus.

"It's too hot to work," answered Angus. "I'm going swimming. Does anybody want to join me?"

"On a hot day like today? You don't have to ask me twice!" answered Alexander.

"Meet you at the stream!" shouted Angus.

Everyone made a beeline for home to fetch towels, blankets, and what they would wear.

They had to drive the cattle and horses from the stream, a challenging task. The animals kept breaking away and coming back. Finally, they succeeded in claiming the stream for themselves.

"How are we going to do it?" asked Kate.

"The men and boys will go downstream and give you womenfolk privacy. Keep the lads and lasses with you," answered Angus.

"Are you men doing what I think you're doing?" asked Kate.

The smile on his face told her the answer.

"Land sakes! Skinny-dipping! You better go downstream!" she ordered.

"We will, Kate, I promise," answered Angus.

Angus rode on and found a promising deep pool.

"This is as good a place as any," he said while dismounting.

Shucking his clothes, he took off running. "Last one in is a bow-legged squaw!" he shouted as he jumped in. Surfacing, he smiled, "Mighty fine! The water feels good!"

In no time, the pool was full of laughing, naked men. That is, all except one.

Angus spotted Little Angus on the bank. He was still fully dressed and had an apprehensive look on his face.

"What's wrong? Aren't you coming in?" asked Angus.

"Pa, I brought a rope with me. I thought I would make a rope swing from that cottonwood branch. It might be fun swinging out over the water and diving in."

"Mighty thoughtful of you," answered Angus. "Do you need any help?"

"No, Pa, I've never seen a tree I couldn't climb."

Angus went back to enjoying the water and forgot about Little Angus. A few minutes later, he heard Abner scream as he swung over the pool. With a mighty splash, Abner belly-flopped into the pool.

The pool emptied in a hurry. Everyone wanted a turn and jostled each other for the rope. Angus quickly put a stop to it. He took the rope in both hands, and with a scream any Indian would be proud of, he swung out over the pool, let loose, and hit the water with a mighty splash.

As Angus climbed out of the pool, he noticed Little Angus sitting on a log, watching them.

"Boy, you still have your clothes on! Aren't you coming in?"

"Pa, you know I can't swim," he answered.

"You can't? I thought all of my boys could swim."

"Nope! Not me," he answered.

Angus got a grin on his face. Turning to his sons. He shouted, "Little Angus can't swim!"

Suddenly, his brothers were heading his way. Little Angus saw them coming, and fear crossed his face. He turned to run, but it was too late. They chased him down and stripped him.

GOING SWIMMING

They had an epic fight on their hands. Little Angus kicked, bit, gouged, and punched to get away. It did no good. There were too many of them.

"Shall we?" shouted Angus.

His answer came quickly. They picked him up, carried him to the stream, and unceremoniously threw him in.

Little Angus came to the surface in a hurry. He was sputtering, spitting stream water, and crying all at the same time.

"Help me! I'll die!" screamed Little Angus.

Angus's answer was immediate, "Sink or swim!"

"I don't know how!"

"Take your arms and reach out like you're grabbing something. Kick your feet!"

Little Angus was terrified. As hard as he was trying, he wasn't going anywhere.

"C'mon, boy, you can do it," shouted Angus as he watched Little Angus's progress. "Ansel, fetch me a stick."

As Little Angus worked his way toward shore, Angus got ready. When Little Angus got close, he held him off with a willow branch.

"Pa, what are you doing?" he screamed.

"I'm teaching you how to swim."

"You're trying to drown me!"

Angus ignored him. Every time he got close, he held

him off until Angus could see that he was getting tired.

"Come on in," he urged.

Little Angus struggled toward the bank, and his brothers helped him ashore.

"Pa, why did you do it? Why did you push me away?"

Angus smiled at him and shook his head, "Boy, that's how all of you learned to swim. It's how I learned."

"I don't understand. I thought you were being mean."

"Boy, you may not realize this. You swam to shore."

"I did?"

"You sure did!"

"I can swim!" shouted Little Angus with glee.

Angus took him by the hand, and they jumped back into the pool.

As he lay that night in Kate's arms, he spoke. "Little Angus learned how to swim today."

"He did? Good for him. Did you teach him?" asked Kate.

"I taught him the way my pa taught me."

Kate shuddered at the thought.

"You're not going to teach me," she muttered.

"You can't swim?"

"Now, just you never mind," she replied.

"We're going swimming tomorrow!" smiled Angus.

"I'll whomp you good!" she threatened.

"Now, Kate, everybody should know how to swim."

"I'm not everybody!"

"I can't wait for tomorrow," he teased as he kissed her goodnight.

"Angus, I'm warning you!" she said while kissing him goodnight.

"You and me are going swimming with the catfish tomorrow. I can't wait."

Kate elbowed him in the ribs.

A LIFE SHARED

It was poker night, and the boys were at the table counting their money. Outside, it was pouring down rain. Between lightning strikes, Angus spoke.

"So, you want to know about my upbringing?"

"Pa, we know a little bit. Ma has told us some, but not very much."

Angus lit his pipe and thought about it. Some of his memories were good, and some were almighty bad.

"I can't see any harm in it," said Angus. "What do you want to know?"

"We want to know it all," answered Ansel.

"You know that I was born in 1800. My pa leased a farm. If that is what you want to call it. Pa rented the farm from a wealthy laird near Argyll in Scotland. It was dirt-poor and rock-rich, and we were starving. Pa happened to go to the pub and heard something about opportunities in America. He came home all excited. All my pa could talk about was free land in America. Once my pa has a notion, you might as well give up trying to change his mind."

"Reminds me of someone we all know," teased Abner.

The look on Angus's face told him he had better be quiet.

"Now, where was I?" he said. "You made me lose my

thoughts."

"Your pa wanted to come to America," answered Little Angus.

"We boarded ship in Glasgow and almost didn't get here. We should have thrown the captain overboard! The ship was filthy, the food was rotten, and people were getting sick and dying. We buried my brother, Ewan, at sea. Ma and Pa took it almighty hard."

"Where did you land?" asked one of the boys.

"We came ashore at Charleston, South Carolina. We were almighty glad that we did. The voyage was a nightmare, but we had made it to America."

"What did you do then?" asked Atticus.

"Pa found a tavern and began asking questions. At first, no one would help us. We were from another country. We didn't know anyone here. We had no clue what to do, where to go, or how to do it. While Pa was in the tavern, someone overheard him talking. He followed Pa out in the street and started talking to him. He told Pa he was heading for Tennessee. He said that maybe the two families could travel together. Said there was safety in numbers. Pa thought about it and agreed.

"Who was the family?" asked Abraham.

The McKinnons was their name. There were six of them in the family. Ma, Pa, two sons, and two daughters. You might know one of the daughters. Her name is Katherine."

"Are you telling us it was Ma?" asked Little Angus.

Angus got a smile on his face as he remembered. "I was eleven, and she was ten. Katherine was and still is the bonniest thing I ever saw. On the way to Tennessee, I couldn't take my eyes off her. Four years later, we tied the knot."

"Pa, you've never told us any of this before," said Ansel.

"I knew the time would come when you would want to know. I guess now is the time," answered Angus. "The McKinnons' land and ours sat beside each other. We built a cabin in the back of the farms, half on McKinnon land and half on ours. We settled in and started having bairns. I didn't have a dollar to my name, but we were happy. Ansel, you were born the following year."

"When did you start trapping?" asked Absalom.

"I tried farming first. I spent many a day hauling rocks and building fences. I broke the ground with a one-bottom plow I borrowed from a neighbor. I quickly discovered that farming wasn't for me. My love was the woods. Hunting, fishing, and chasing critters always won out. I set my first trap when I was seventeen. I never touched another plow from that moment on," Angus told his sons.

"Were you able to make a living?" asked Atticus.

A LIFE SHARED

"I did right well for myself," answered Angus. "I had some hounds that weren't afraid of anything. I killed my fair share of bears and painters. Folks heard about me and got the word to me to come if a critter was a problem. That's how I was able to put food on the table. By the time I came west, there were five of you: Ansel, Atticus, Anne, Abraham, and Abigail. You were born a year apart from each other. Your ma had trouble birthing Abraham and Abigail since they are twins."

"Pa, why didn't you give us Scottish names?"

"Your ma and I talked about it. She wanted to, and I thought otherwise. We were making a new start here, and I didn't want you tied down with names people would have a hard time saying."

The brothers nodded in agreement.

"What made you decide to go trapping?" asked Little Angus.

"I heard about the beaver trade and the money that I could make, and I couldn't pass it up," answered Angus.

"Who did you trap with?" asked Absalom.

"I joined Jim Bridger's brigade when I was twenty-one years old. I heard he was looking for trappers, and your ma and I talked. Kate's ma and pa and mine would look after your ma and you. So, we made the decision. Leaving my family was hard, but it was for the best."

"When did you find the Glen?" asked Abner.

"I found it in 1823. I was scouting for beaver and found the valley then. I knew right then and there I would someday live here, and it happened. By God, it happened," he answered.

"Pa, when did you meet the Lord?" asked Little Angus.

"Jedediah Smith led me to Him. He was a God-fearing man. Jedediah didn't cuss or drink. He never bedded an Indian woman. I took a liking to Jedediah, and he told me about God. I wanted to be like him. I surely did. I will never forget Jedediah Smith. Indians killed him on the way to Santa Fe."

"How often did you come home?" asked Ansel.

"Every chance I got. I made it a point to get home after trapping season. It usually was for about a month, and then I had to get back. We had six more babies through the years, not counting the ones we lost. By my count, there should be sixteen of you."

"Sixteen? Pa, what happened?" exclaimed Little Angus.

"You will have to ask the good Lord when you meet Him face to face," Angus answered.

"Did you go to the rondyvoos?" asked Abraham.

"I went to all of them. I went there to resupply. I didn't get caught up in any of the rowdiness. By that time, the

A LIFE SHARED

Lord and I were on a first-name basis. While they were getting drunk, I was telling the other trappers about the Lord," answered Angus.

"Did they listen to you?"

"Some did, and some didn't. I knew I wouldn't win all of the trappers. Whenever something went wrong, they would come to me. I'd pray for them and let God take care of it. That is how I got my name. To this day, most of them know me as "Preacher," said their Pa.

"Pa, did you do good trapping?" asked Alexander.

"I was as good a trapper as the best of them. I've caught hundreds of beaver while trapping. I was different from most of my friends. I saved my money and brought it home to your ma. She used what she needed and put the rest away. That's why six of you have birthdays so close together. When the time came, I had the money for us to make the move. We sold that worthless piece of rocky ground and came here."

"You had to have saved a lot for us to come," offered Abner.

"I did alright for myself. I'm going to tell you a secret. I kept my eye out for gold in those streams while setting traps. I would find some from time to time. One day, I found a ledge that showed color. The more I dug into it, the more I found. I had to keep it from my trapping buddies.

McDougal's Glen

Men would have killed me for it. When trapping was over for the season, I always went to the ledge and dug. I had to be careful that nobody followed me. I always went out of my way to get to the ledge. I also had to watch out for the Indians. They would have lifted my hair." confided Angus.

"How much did you find?" asked a curious Little Angus.

"Over seven hundred pounds. Your ma survived on the money the beaver plews brought and saved the gold."

"It was a fortune!" gasped Alexander.

"Aye, it was."

"Were you ever scared?" asked Little Angus.

"What kind of tom fool question is that? I've been scared many times. A man can't spend all those years out here without having the daylights scared out of him," answered Angus.

"Indians?" asked one of the boys.

"I've had scrapes with all of them."

"Who were the meanest?"

"Down Texas way, it was the Comanches. Up in these parts, It was the Crows and Blackfeet. You couldn't trust any of them," Angus gave his opinion.

"Critters?"

"I've had my fair share of critters. I had to take on a griz with only my knife," Angus said while pulling up his shirt to show the scars, "Me and a lion were in the same tree one day. It was no fun at all. There wasn't room for both of us. It lay dead at the foot of the tree come morning."

"Did you ever have to whomp anybody?" asked Abraham.

"I've busted a few heads. My friends knew I wouldn't put up with God's name used in a bad way. After I knocked some sense into them, they were careful what they said around me."

"Did you have anyone you didn't want any truck with?"

"I had a few. One man always rises to the top."

"Who was it?" asked Little Angus.

"Liver-Eating Johnson. You couldn't trust him. He was almighty mean and wanted to be alone. I was happy to oblige him."

"Pa, did you ever kill a man?" asked Abner.

Angus settled back in his chair and closed his eyes. He had tears in his eyes when he opened them. "Yes, and I'm not proud of it. Taking a life is a serious thing not to be taken lightly. I have been in situations where it was me or them, and I had no choice. Some men needed killing, and they brought it on themselves. Whether it was Indians or white men, their doings sealed their fate. You boys have been with me and seen it happen. When I could, I prayed for them before they went under. I know I led a few of them to the Lord on their deathbed. I can still see their faces in my mind. It's something a person never gets over; at least, I never will."

"Pa, I'm sorry I brought it up," said Abner. "I should have left it alone."

"Abner, it's all right. It's part of life and needs talking about. Let's talk about something else before it starts raining again."

"Pa, you led a downright interesting life," said Atticus. "Would you do it over again?"

Angus paused and spoke. "Those were the best days of my life. I would have to say yes. I would jump at the chance if I was young and offered the opportunity. Once you smell the fresh mountain air, drink from an ice-cold stream, and eat your first buffalo hump, you never forget it. It makes you a man. Nobody can tell you what it's like until you've experienced it. You feel free to do as you wish whenever you want to. Going wherever you want and not having anyone tell you what to do is mighty satisfying."

"Pa, you make it sound wonderful," sighed Abner.

"It was wonderful," answered Angus as he went to the door. "It looks like the rain's stopped. You boys better get home to your families."

"You told them all of that?" asked Kate.

"Yes, Kate, I did."

"You couldn't keep a secret if your life depended on it!" teased Kare.

"Now, Kate, they had a right to know. Don't you want our lads and lasses to know anything about us?"

"I reckon you're right," answered Kate. "You didn't tell them about our shivaree, did you?"

"I thought about it," he teased.

"You old coot! I'll whomp you good!"

"Now, Kate, would you do that?"

Rolling over, she said, "Good night."

"Good night, Kate," Angus said with a smile.

McDougal's Glen

SPOOKED!

"Pa, what is it?" asked Abraham.

"I don't rightly know," answered Angus while reining in his horse.

"Kinda spooky!" shuddered Abner.

Angus and his two sons were checking on the herd in a box canyon called Shadows. They had left the ranch house at daybreak, nooned at a stream they called Shining Waters, and they entered the canyon. The moment they entered, a feeling came over them that they were being watched. It was a different feeling than Skeleton Canyon, where Hairy Man lived. This feeling was evil. As they went deeper into the canyon, Angus stopped and motioned for his sons to do likewise.

"Check your rifles! Make sure you haven't lost your prime. I don't like the feeling I'm getting. My knower knows something isn't right. The hair on my neck is standing up and waving attention. Keep your eyes peeled. We may have to skedaddle out of here!" he ordered.

"Pa, I don't like this none at all!" whispered Abraham. "I have a feeling something doesn't want us here."

"Me too, Pa, let's get out of here. We can come back with all of us. There's safety in numbers," added Abner.

"Now, just sit tight for a spell. Maybe we can make

SPOOKED!

some sense of this. I don't like it either. But I'll not lift my tail and run without knowing why. Let's get up on that ridge over yonder and take a look, see around us."

As they got to the ridge, they began finding peculiar things.

"Look here, Pa," said Abraham. "I've never seen the like!"

They reined up in front of a circle made out of longhorn skulls. Something or someone had placed the heads inside with the horns pointing out. It was a large circle with fourteen heads perfectly placed.

"What do you think, Pa?" whispered Abner.

"I'm thinking some lowlife has helped himself to our cattle," Angus answered.

"But why would anybody go to the effort to do this?" questioned Abner.

"Pa, cutting their heads off would be a chore. The shoulder and neck muscles are like bands of iron. I surely wouldn't want to do it," offered Abraham.

It's a mystery, that's for sure," replied Angus. "Let's get up on that ridge. Let's see what we can see."

Once on top, Angus took out his spyglass and studied the canyon. Off in the distance, he could see longhorns. The more he watched them, the more befuddled he became. There was something almighty wrong. Handing his spyglass to Abner, he asked him, "What do you see?"

Abner watched for a few minutes and answered Angus, "Pa, something's got them spooked."

"Let me take a look," said Abraham.

He watched and said, "They're standing in a circle facing out as if they expect trouble. I don't see any critters around them. You know they'd hightail it out of there if it was a bear or cougar. I don't see hide nor hair of a wolf either."

"Pa, you know longhorns aren't afraid of anything. They'd go head-to-head with Lucifer if they had to," said Abner.

"Let's get down there. We can't figure anything out up here," ordered Angus.

They agreed and started down the ridge. As they rode, Angus was convinced they were being watched. The thing was, he couldn't spot anybody. All the years on the frontier had heightened his senses. Angus knew how to conceal himself and knew where to look for somebody. It bothered him, bothered him a lot.

Stranger things were discovered the closer they came to the herd. The men started finding the headless skeletons of their cattle. The carcasses had been picked clean by something. The men couldn't find blood, guts, or hides anywhere.

SPOOKED!

"Any ideas?" asked Abner.

Angus ignored him. He was too busy looking for signs, and he saw none. There were no footprints or anything to help him. Moving on, they entered some trees and stopped in their tracks. Hanging from the branches were strips of cowhide. A gentle breeze was blowing, causing them to flutter in the wind. The fluttering spooked their horses, and it was all the men could do to control them.

"What are we going to do?" asked Abner.

"I want to see the cattle up close," answered Angus.

The problem was they couldn't get close. Each group of cattle they approached bawled, rolled their eyes, and took off running.

"What's got them spooked? I've seen them like this during a bad lightning storm. These critters are scared something fierce," said Abner while watching them run.

"Don't know. I'll have to think on it some," answered Angus. "Fill your canteens from the creek over there. We'll camp on that ridge overnight."

They filled their canteens and retreated to the ridge. They found a defendable place to bed down in a pile of rocks. Angus hobbled the horses while Abraham and Abner gathered firewood.

"I reckon that's enough." chuckled Angus as he watched them carry armload after armload to the fire. "Are you scared? Think the banshees will get you?"

The boys knew what banshees were. Their pa had filled their heads full of stories about Scotland and banshees. When they were little, he had scared all of them with stories about the night and what roamed around.

"Hush, Pa," they both answered him.

After a supper of cold biscuits and jerky, they lit their pipes and talked.

"Pa, have you ever seen a banshee or heard one?"

"Can't say that I have. Why?"

"Just wondering. How about Grandpap?" the two inquired.

"Well, he said he heard one when he was a lad. He heard the banshee scream on a cold and windy night. He said his pa went to the door, peeked out, slammed it shut, latched it, and began reading his Bible. He found out the next day that his neighbor died just about when he heard the banshee scream."

Abner and Abraham shuddered while looking at each other.

"Abner, you take the first watch, then you, Abraham. I'll do the last one. Wake me up around three," Angus ordered.

Towards midnight, Angus jumped to his feet at the report of a gunshot. Abraham joined him. They went

SPOOKED!

looking for Abner.

"Why did you fire a shot?" asked Angus.

"Pa, there's something out there. I could hear it moving around," answered Abner.

Angus could see that Abner was worried.

"Did you see anything?"

"No, Pa, but I know there's something out there."

In the distance, they could hear cattle bawling. And then the cattle were running.

"No use checking on the cattle tonight. It's too dark. Abraham, it's your turn to stand watch."

At that moment, a scream pierced the night air. It was nothing like anything they had heard before. It sounded like it was all around them.

"What in tarnation?" whispered Angus.

The scream turned to a howl, the howl getting louder by the minute, undulating with its ferocity.

"Pa, what is it?"

"I don't know! Let's get back to the fire!" he ordered.

They spent the rest of the night with their backs against a rock. They piled the fire high with wood until it was a bonfire.

"Boys, the only thing I know to do is pray. We have to trust that God will protect us. All I can think about is the twenty-third psalm. Say it with me, please?" asked Angus.

McDougal's Glen

As they began, a peace came over them. The howl stopped, and they were relieved. Angus didn't want to admit he was as shaken as his boys. He kept thinking about the stories from his childhood.

Dawn finally broke. The men fixed a meager breakfast, saddled up, and headed for the canyon's entrance. They found a freshly killed longhorn lying in the middle of the trail; its head was gone, and the ravens were picking the bones clean. One look was all it took. They spurred their horses and skedaddled!

He sat at the fire in Beaver Tail's village a week later.

"It takes a lot to spook me," Angus told his friend," but this got to me."

Beaver Tail listened and grinned, "What canyon was it?"

Angus told him, and Beaver Tail nodded.

"You were in the Little People's Canyon. We have known about the Little People for as long as we can remember. Our elders passed stories down about them. My people will not go there. No one goes there. They must flee if they do. Did they howl?"

Angus nodded yes.

"That is their warning for you to leave. Anyone who doesn't will pay a price. Long ago, a hunting party camped there. They never came home. We found their horses running free and caught them. We found the men. Their bones were lying in a circle. We never did find their heads. The men who found the hunting party said they were sure they were being watched. Don't go back, my friend. Your cattle aren't worth your lives."

"Why didn't you tell me about them when we first came here?" asked Angus.

"Your valley is big. I didn't think you would use that canyon."

Angus nodded and left.

A week later, Angus led thirty men into the canyon. The party had camped a couple of miles outside the canyon. At daybreak, they rode in, intending on driving every longhorn they could find out of the canyon before nightfall. Some of them wanted to stay overnight and see if anything would happen. Angus quickly nipped that idea in the bud. He showed them the ring of skulls.

"Do you want to take a chance and have your skeletons lying there instead of the longhorn skulls?" he asked.

That changed everyone's minds fast. The men got the longhorns out of the canyon and started home.

Angus was the last man out of the canyon. He turned once more to see if they had missed any cattle. He screamed, and his horse reared in terror. Standing before him was a little man holding a shillelagh.

Angus lit a shuck for home!

LITTLE PEOPLE

Angus and Kate were in bed, and she nestled on his shoulder, her long gray hair billowing around her head like a crown. Kate was laughing hysterically.

"You saw what?" she gasped between guffaws.

"You heard me. I saw a little man. It liked to scare me to death. My horse went loco on me. I thought it was going to throw me. Sure enough glad it didn't. I'd probably have shillelagh knots on my head!"

That brought another round of laughter from Kate.

"You old coot! If I didn't know you better, I'd say you've been hitting the corn squeezings!"

"Now Kate, you know better than that," he answered. "As crazy as it sounds, I can't rightly figure it out. You should have heard the scream. Grandpap said it was something he would never forget. I surely won't, either. I still can't figure out how such a big scream could come out of a man no more than three feet tall!"

"So, you're not making it up?" she asked.

"Have you ever known me to be scared of anything except your skillet when you're riled up?"

Kate got quiet. After a few minutes, she answered him.

"No, by gum, can't say that I have. When you're mad enough, you'd take on old Lucifer himself."

LITTLE PEOPLE

"Kate, that scream done shook me up. I can't say I ever want to go back there. I'm figuring on putting up a sign saying, 'Stay Out!'"

She listened while he told her what Beaver Tail had said about his tribe staying away from the canyon and how they knew about the Little People.

"And you believed him?" she asked.

"I saw one with my own two eyes! That's good enough for me!"

They went to sleep, and about midnight, they sat straight up in bed, holding each other tight. What woke them up was the awfullest scream either of them had ever heard.

"What is it?" asked a terrified Kate.

"It's the same scream the boys and I heard at the canyon. It's the Little People! They followed us here!"

"What are we going to do?" cried Kate as she clung to Angus.

"I don't rightly know. I'll get my rifle and have a look," answered Angus.

"Don't leave me," Kate whispered. "I hear banshees can be frightful mean."

"You had better come with me then," he answered.

Angus and Kate slipped their feet into moccasins, cracked the door, and peeked out. They didn't see a thing.

McDougal's Glen

Angus crept toward the barn with Kate hanging onto his shirttail. They opened the barn door, and the scream started all over again. Angus shuddered, almost dropped his rifle, and hightailed it for the house with Kate behind him. They bolted through the door and dropped the barricade bar in place.

Meanwhile, laughter erupted from the loft. Abner and Abraham watched as their ma and pa skedaddled for the house.

"I've never seen Ma and Pa move so fast!" laughed Abner.

"Me either. That scream sure enough hurt my throat. But it was worth it! It surely was," giggled Abraham.

"Pa will skin us alive if he finds out!" laughed Abner.

"Who's going to tell him? I'm not!" said Abner.

"Do it again tomorrow night?" asked Abner.

"Why not! Nothing wrong with having a little fun," snorted Abraham through muffled laughs.

"Amen, brother, amen!" chimed the two in unison.

Meanwhile, at the ranch house, sheer panic reigned. Angus loaded every gun he had and placed them at the doors and windows. Kate backed herself into a corner and cried, a butcher knife in one hand and her cast-iron skillet in the other.

"What are we gonna do if it gets in here?" she cried.

"I'll shoot it, and you whomp it with your skillet. We had better pray," said Angus.

He joined her in the corner. They bowed their heads and began.

Meanwhile, the boys split up and headed for home. Abraham crawled into bed and chuckled as he thought about what they had done. He woke up later with a sore throat. Needing a drink of water, Abraham got up and went to the kitchen, found the water pitcher, and poured a tin cup full when he caught a motion out of the corner of his eye. What he saw made him drop his cup and scream.

Outlined by the moon, a little man peered in the window at him. He lifted his shillelagh into the air and screamed.

Abraham fainted!

BEAR PROBLEMS

"Pa, you had better come quick. We've got problems!" shouted Ansel.

"What kind of problems?" asked Angus while rising from his rocker on the porch.

"Bear problems. A grizzly got one of the colts last night."

"Where?"

"Down by the lake. We noticed a mare pawing the ground and circling something. The closer we got, it was obvious it was a colt's remains. We found tracks. The grizzly is a big one. I've never seen tracks as big as these," answered Ansel.

"Let me get my rifle and pouch. Send Abner after the dogs. We'll probably have to track it."

"I'll fetch him."

Angus saddled his horse and followed his sons to the lake. The mare was still there, smelling the remains, stomping her feet, her eyes wide with fear.

"She smells the bear. I'm surprised she hasn't hightailed it out of here," said Angus as he dismounted.

Leaning over the tracks, he could put his hand inside one with room to spare.

"We have to kill it. Once a bear gets the taste of

horseflesh, it never forgets it. This beast will deliberately stalk our horses. We can't have that bear killing our horses. No sir, we can't."

Rising to his feet, he looked off in the direction the tracks headed.

"This won't be easy," he thought. "That bear's not stupid. He's probably watching his back trail, so we have to be careful."

"Abner, bring the dogs over here," ordered Angus.

The closer they got, the more excited they became. Abner was having a hard time holding them. They were a pair of hounds they brought with them from Tennessee. Blue Tick hounds that had been on many a bear trail. Now, the hounds had worked themselves into a frenzy, wanting that bear.

"Let them get a good smell!" Angus ordered.

Abner let them have a long smell, and Angus shouted, "Turn them loose!"

He did, and off they raced. The bear was wary. It had headed for the roughest terrain, a jumble of rocks and fallen pine trees. It was a place only a man could get through. There was no way a horse could get through that jumbled mess.

"Boys, listen to me," ordered Angus. "There's nothing more dangerous than a grizzly bear unless it's a wounded one. Grizzlies, at a short distance, are as fast as Banshee. I know because I had one come after me. If it hadn't been for Whiskey Jack, I wouldn't be here today."

"What do we do?"

They could hear the dogs ahead. Suddenly, the baying changed into excited yipping and howls.

"They've got the bear cornered. Better hurry. That bruin will kill the dogs if we're not there to stop it," shouted Angus.

They took off at a dead run, weaving in and out of the rocks, running toward the fight ahead. They stopped when they heard a dog yelp in pain, and the chase started again.

"We may be too late. Watch your step," shouted Angus as he scrambled over rocks and downed trees.

They found the dog, and it was in bad shape. It was lying on its side. The hound whined when they tried to move it, revealing deep lacerations on its side, and one ear was dangling by a thin strip of bloody skin. Abner took a piece of an old blanket from his pouch and wrapped the dog, hoping he could stop the bleeding.

"Abner, you stay with the dog. Ansel and I will go," ordered Angus.

Climbing a ridge, they stopped and listened. In the distance, they could hear the dog, still baying and in hot pursuit.

"Let's go! Time's wasting!"

They took off in a fast trot. Again, they heard the excited barking of the dog in the distance.

"We can't lose another dog. Better hurry up!"

Up ahead was a rugged pile of rocks. The ruckus was coming from there.

"Slow down. You don't rush up on a grizzly, especially a mad one. Follow my lead," ordered Angus.

Angus felt for his hunting knife. He was relieved to find that he hadn't lost it. Then Angus double-checked his rifle. Satisfied, he set his bag down and took off his coat. Angus replaced his boots with moccasins from his bag. He motioned for Ansel to do the same.

"Let's go."

They entered the pile of rocks, their senses on edge and ready for anything. Angus glimpsed a movement. The bear was on them, knocking Ansel down with a mighty swat with its paw, roaring and biting as it stood over him.

Angus tried to get off a shot but couldn't. Because of the awkward position he was in, he might hit Ansel. Ansel screamed as the bear bit into his thigh with its massive jaws and began to rip his flesh.

Angus dropped his rifle, pulled his knife, and waded in. Seeing his chance, Angus plunged his knife into the bear's side. Roaring with pain, it let loose of Ansel and turned to face Angus. Coming for him, Angus braced himself for the impact. Behind the bear, he saw the dog charging. The hound nipped the bear's flank, and the bear turned toward the hound. Angus stabbed the bear again, plunging the blade repeatedly into its side. Blood gushed down his hand and forearm. The bear roared and started to turn around when something incredible happened. The dog launched itself at the bear's throat. Latching on, the dog hung there as the bear shook its head with fury. It was desperately trying to shake the dog loose. Angus plunged his knife deep into the bear's back. Roaring, it again turned to face Angus when the gun went off. It became a dead grizzly.

Angus looked behind him and found Ansel with his smoking rifle in his hands. He had rolled over and grabbed his pa's gun.

"Whew! I thought I was a goner!" sighed Angus.

"Me too!" answered Ansel.

"Are you hurt bad?"

"My leg's in bad shape."

"Think you can walk?"

"I don't know. I may need some help."

"I'll get Abner. Stay put. We'll be back soon."

While he waited, Ansel admired the bear. It was massive and in its prime. As he sat there, the dog came to him. It wagged its tail and licked his face. It had a few tiny cuts on its ears and sides. Other than that, it was all right.

"Good boy," he said as he hugged it.

Angus and Abner came back in a few minutes. They bandaged his leg and cut a primitive crutch. Ansel wasn't in any physical danger. The men skinned the bear, carved the best pieces of bear meat to take back, and began the journey home. Ansel was too weak from loss of blood. The men made a travois to transport him and the injured dog home. It was a long, slow ride back to the ranch.

Later, after they had doctored Ansel and put him in bed, Angus sat by the fire and thought about the day's happenings.

"Almost lost one of my boys today," he thought. "Kate would have never forgiven me, let alone Priscilla and the boys."

He lit his pipe and sat in silence. He heard footsteps come up behind him. A pair of arms encircled his neck and hugged him. Immediately, Angus knew who it was.

"Is he all right?"

"He's running a high fever. Pricilla's with him now. We think he'll be all right," came the answer.

"Sit with me, Kate. I need some company tonight."

She came around and sat down beside him. Laying her head on his shoulder, she waited.

"Almost lost him today," he softly spoke. "I don't know what I would have done if it had happened. How could I face Priscilla?"

"That's the chance we take living here. You know the risks. Death happens every day. It's hard, but you have to deal with it. The boys are strong, and you have taught them well. That's all you can do," she offered.

"I know," he replied. "I just love my family too much to lose any of them."

"Angus, that bear could have killed you. How could we go on without you?" she asked while holding him tight.

"Never crossed my mind. The only thing I thought about was saving Ansel."

"I know. You brought Ansel home. That is all that matters," she said while punching him in the ribs.

"Are you sure about that?"

"Yes, I am! Let's go to bed," she answered.

Taking his hand in hers, she said, "Tomorrow's another day."

"Yes, dear."

JOSEPH

Angus had just lit his pipe and settled into his rocker. The afternoon sun warmed his bones and did wonders for his aching knees. Many years of wading bone-chilling streams and setting beaver traps had caused his arthritis to flare up.

Now that he was over seventy years old, Angus found his rocker where he could ease the pain he felt. The warmth and a full belly produced one thing as he sat there. He dozed off. He was jolted awake in the middle of a dream about Kate and their shivaree.

"Pa!" shouted Little Angus. "Beaver Tail and what looks like a war party are across the river. You had better come."

Angus glared at him and spoke. "Boy, I was having a good dream, and you stopped it. I reckon I better see what he wants."

Angus grabbed his cane and got up. Little Angus had saddled his horse and helped him mount up. They went through the cave and down to the river.

"Ahhhngus!" shouted Beaver Tail above the roar of the rushing water.

"Beaver Tail!" shouted Angus while motioning for him to cross over.

Beaver Tail and a handful of braves crossed and approached him. Angus couldn't help but notice that a man rode beside his friend. He didn't recognize him, but something told him the man was important.

"Beaver Tail, old friend, it is good to see you," he offered out loud while doing sign language so the man with Beaver Tail would understand.

"Ahhhngus," he said, "we need your help."

"What can I do?" he answered.

"Ahhhngus," he said while turning to the man. "This is Joseph of the Wal-lam-wat-kain band of my tribe, the Nez Perce."

Angus acknowledged the man by using sign language.

"Joseph," he said. "I am Angus McDougal. This is my home, and you are welcome here."

Joseph studied him for a few moments and nodded. "Beaver Tail has told me about you. How you have helped his people."

"Yes, I have done that. Beaver Tail and I are like brothers," replied Angus.

"He has told me that. It is good that he trusts you. Not many white men can we trust. Can I trust you?" Joseph answered with a question in his voice.

Angus stared at him and made a quick decision. If they were going to stay on peaceful terms with the Nez Perce, he would have to take a chance.

"Joseph, my answer is yes. Can I trust you?" asked Angus while looking him in the eyes.

"We will smoke and talk," he answered, reaching into his pouch fastened around his horse's neck. Pulling out a pipe and a rawhide bag of kinnikinnick, specially blended with herbs, barks, and plant matter.

"Follow me," said Angus, turning his horse around and heading for the cave. They rode through and out onto the bench. He could tell that Joseph was impressed.

They rode down to the stream and found a place to sit under the shade of a cottonwood tree. Angus built a fire and waited. Joseph filled the pipe and lit it from the fire. Taking a deep drag, he handed it to Beaver Tail. Beaver Tail did the same and offered it to Angus. They kept passing the pipe until they had consumed the mixture and the ashes went out.

Angus knew this meant something was about to happen, and he must wait.

"Ahhhngus," said Beaver Tail. "We, the Nez Perce, are worried about our future. Every day, more whites come here and take our land. Our home is here. As long as our elders can remember, we have lived here."

"Beaver Tail, what you say is true. Because of our friendship, you have allowed me and my family to live here peacefully. What will happen next, I don't know."

"If it comes to war, will you fight with the whites?" asked Beaver Tail.

The question surprised Angus, and he paused before answering. "Beaver Tail, I will never lift my hand against you and your people. The only way such a thing could happen is if you betray our friendship and hurt my family."

"Will you help the soldiers?"

"No. If the soldiers ask me to scout for them, I will refuse. I am getting too old to scout. That will be my reason to say no."

Beaver Tail nodded, turned to Joseph, and said, "You can trust Angus. I owe him my life."

Young Joseph nodded and spoke. "In my heart, I know I will lead my people one day. A dream told me this. I promise that no harm will come to you when I become chief. I give you my word."

The men rose, mounted, and rode back through the cave and down to the river.

"Ahhhngus, my friend," Beaver Tail shouted as he crossed the river. "We will meet again."

Angus waved as they rode away. Returning to the ranch house, he thought about the meeting. Little did he know how important that meeting was for him and his family.

Conflicts flared up with the Nez Perce as the territory

filled up with settlers. He began hearing about raids and depredations against the settlers. These things happened around the glen but never in it or to the McDougals.

Angus remembered when the cavalry came riding up to the Trading Post.

"Are you Angus McDougal?" asked the officer.

"Aye," he answered.

"Have you had any Indian problems?"

"No, I can't say we have," answered Angus.

"That's strange. I wonder why? We're after Chief Joseph's band of Nez Perce," said the officer.

"I haven't seen them," Angus answered, shrugging his shoulders.

"If you do, send word to me," ordered the officer.

Angus nodded and waved as they rode away.

That night, as Kate was lying in his arms, he spoke. "Cavalry was here today."

"What did they want?" asked Kate.

"They're looking for Chief Joseph's band," replied Angus.

"What did you tell them?"

"I told them I haven't seen them."

"Angus! Shame on you! You know they've been camping down by the stream."

"They have?" said Angus with a mischievous look.

"You old coot! You better pray about your lie!"

"Kate," he said, "I didn't lie. I haven't seen them today."

She glared at him and grumbled, "good night," as she rolled over and went to sleep.

Angus prayed, "Father, forgive me for lying to protect the Nez Perce. It seems like they are always getting cheated. I ask that you help the Nez Perce tribe. They are good people. All they want is to be left alone on the land they love. Amen."

Angus began hearing about the plight of the Nes Perce. It broke his heart when they finally surrendered.

Little did Angus know that Chief Joseph would die with a broken heart in 1904.

RONDYVOO

"Now, what are the old coots up to?" murmured Kate as she got up from her rocker.

In the distance, she could hear gunfire, and she was worried. Going to the door, she stepped out on the porch and turned her attention towards the woods by the stream. Kate could see the colorful row of teepees and the corral full of horses. She could also see a group of buckskin-clad men standing around a roaring fire.

Kate couldn't help but think back to the day last fall when Angus crawled into bed and snuggled up against her. She knew that something was going through his mind when he put his head on her shoulder and began holding her hand. She knew that all she had to do was wait.

"Kate, honey, I've been thinking about something," Angus whispered.

"And what might that be?" she asked.

"I'm thinking about having a rondyvoo," Angus answered with a faraway look in his eye.

"Angus McDougal! Have you been drinking?"

"I'm serious. There aren't many of us left. I sure would like to see my friends again," Angus countered.

"Another of your silly notions," Kate said while moving out from under his head.

"Why is it silly? What would it hurt? We've got a fine place to have it. Kate, you know several of them. What do you say?" asked Angus.

"A rondyvoo? All that drinking and tomfoolery! Are you sure?"

"We are getting almighty old. I'm figuring they've slowed down some. It would be a passel of fun. Probably be my last chance to see them alive," pondered Angus.

"When are you planning it?" she asked.

"Come spring. Probably in May," he answered.

"Promise me it won't get out of hand," asked Kate.

"Kate, I promise I will do my best to keep it safe," assured Angus.

"I can see it is important to you. You have always given me everything I ever asked for. Angus, I can't say no," whispered Kate.

"Thank you," he smiled.

"Now go to sleep before I change my mind!" Kate ordered as she rolled over.

Angus started by sending letters to the fur buyers in St. Louis. He figured that if anyone knew where the old-timers were, surely they would.

He started getting responses almost immediately. Some of the replies were good, and some brought tears to his eyes. So many of his old friends had gone under, and he

McDougal's Glen

had never had a chance to say a proper goodbye.

The last week of April, Angus and his sons began setting up teepees for the rondyvoo. Beaver Tail had loaned the teepees to him with one request. He wanted to come. Naturally, Angus said yes. Beaver Tail knew many trappers and wanted to see them before he died.

Angus was excited and worried at the same time. Would his friends come? He got his answer when a keelboat pulled up to the Trading Post pier, and a handful of rough-and-tumble frontiersmen stepped ashore.

"Well, I'll be flamboozled, hornswoggled, and dipped in skunk juice!" shouted Angus when he saw them.

"Preacher! How are you?" shouted Kit Carson.

"Good, Kit," beamed Angus. "Who be with you?"

"Seth Kinman, Jim Clyman, Tom Tobin, and Dick Wooten," answered Kit.

"Good to see all of you. Welcome to McDougal's Glen."

In the days that followed, several more trickled in.

"I hear Bridger is coming. He's getting almighty old," said Kit.

"I'd be glad to see him," said Angus.

Joe Meek rode in with Doc Newell, Osborne Russell, Rufus Sage, and Joe Walker.

"Heard you were havin' a rondyvoo," said Meek. "I

knew I had to come. I'm hankerin' for some buff ribs."

"We've got plenty of them. I set the camp up down by the stream," offered Angus.

The men kept coming. Grizzly Adams, Bill Perkins, Robert Campbell, John Brown, and Benjamin Bonneville arrived safely and were ready for the festivities.

Angus received word that Jim Bridger and Jim Breckworth weren't coming. Said they were feeling right poorly. Angus was to tell everyone that they missed them and wished they were there.

There was one more arrival that they turned away. Liver-Eating Johnson showed up. All of the men held a short meeting.

"Don't let him stay," said Kit. "He's nothing but trouble."

"I agree," said Joe Meek. "I don't trust him."

"Nor do I," offered Jim Clyman.

"Then it's settled," said Angus. "Come with me."

The men went to the river's edge and watched as Angus talked to him.

"Johnson," he said, "you had better leave. You are not welcome here."

Looking into Johnson's eyes, they could see a glitter of hatred. He was a dangerous man.

"Is that you talking?" he sneered.

"No, it's all of us," shouted Angus.

Johnson looked at the men, shook his head, and rode away.

"We had better watch our backsides from now on. Johnson can be almighty mean when he's drunk. And especially when he's mad," offered Grizzly Adams.

"I'll have my hired hands keep an eye on him," said Angus.

"My braves will follow him," said Beaver Tail. "He is not wanted here."

The rondyvoo turned out to be one of the best the men ever had. There weren't any Indians wanting to lift their topknots, so all of them could relax.

They sat around the fire and swapped tales. It was hard to tell who was the biggest liar. They had shooting matches, which Angus won, knife and hatchet throwing contests, and horse races. It was a grand time.

Angus told them about Skeleton Canyon, and they called him on it.

"Preacher, you're full of it!" said Jim Baker.

"I never heard of such a thing!" scoffed Rufus Sage.

"I'll take you there tomorrow," offered Angus.

"By gum, you're on!" scoffed the men.

They rode out at daybreak, and all came back that evening believers.

"Did you see the size of that thing?" one of the men asked with a look of awe.

"Bigger than a full-growed grizzly," offered another.

Kit was quiet and then spoke. "I saw one once. I couldn't believe my eyes. An old Blackfoot told me about them. Says they keep themselves out of sight."

Everyone knew that Kit didn't lie. They shook their heads and went away to think about it. Some of them slept that night with one eye open, just in case.

On the last day of the rondyvoo, Angus called them together and spoke.

"I want to show you something. Something I've been working on since I sent out the invite."

"What is it, Angus?"

"Follow me," he said as he mounted his horse.

He led them to a rock formation that stood in a prominent place near the entrance to the valley.

"This is what I wanted you to see," Angus humbly said.

The men dismounted and followed him to the rock.

"My, Angus! What have you done?" asked Kit.

On the rock were chiseled the names of their friends that had gone under.

"Look! There's Hugh Glass's name."

"I see John Colter."

"On this rock is the name of our friends. I will add

McDougal's Glen

more as I hear of their deaths," said Angus.

The men took off their hats and stared in reverence. It was a monument and an everlasting remembrance to honor them.

"Angus, I don't know what to say," said Joe Meek.

"All I ask is that you send word to me when another goes under. I will add it to the rock."

"I'd be glad too," said Kit.

All of the men agreed to do as Angus requested. From his saddlebags, Angus produced some flasks.

"You know I don't imbibe. But let's drink to our friends."

They passed the flasks and rode back to camp.

The rondyvoo ended with the men sharing farewells, bear hugs, and tears. They all knew they might never see each other again.

The evening of the day the men left, Angus and Kate were lying in each other's arms.

"Was it worth it?"

"Kate, you ask some down-right silly questions."

She knew that it had been a time that Angus would never forget.

"I'm glad they came. It was good to see them."

"It sure was. Thank you for letting me do it."

Kate kissed him and answered, "You old coot, you

knew I wouldn't say no."

Smiling, he answered, "Goodnight."

"Goodnight."

THE DREAM

Out of a deep sleep, Angus violently sat up in bed. Flailing his arms, he began mumbling, "My rifle! Give me my rifle!"

Kate jumped up and shouted. "What is it? What's wrong?"

By this time, Angus was wide awake. He was trembling, and sweat beaded his brow.

"I had a dream. It was so real, it downright scared me!"

"Land sakes! You woke me up because of a dream?"

"Kate, I couldn't help it," Angus said while trying to calm down.

"Can you remember it? If so, then tell me about it," Kate asked.

Angus laid back and thought hard about it. He usually couldn't remember his dreams. But this one was different.

"I think I can remember it," he said. "Just be patient with me."

"Anytime you're ready," encouraged Kate.

"As near as I can recollect, I was at a rondyvoo. I don't know which one, so I figure that isn't important."

"Go on," urged Kate.

"The traders had set up their tents and had all of their goods for trade. There was a wagon with barrels of whiskey

THE DREAM

and beer. A long line of trappers was in front of that wagon, and as usual, there was pushing and shoving going on," added Angus.

"Were you in line?" asked Kate.

"Kate, don't stop me. I might lose it," grumbled Angus.

She nodded and listened.

Angus continued, "I wasn't in line. I had just traded beaver plews for a new pair of red flannel long underwear. I remember Kit Carson and Joe Meeks giving me grief over them. I had sat down too close to the fire that morning. I was wearing my old red flannels. I started getting hot and could smell something burning. Come to discover, it was me. My red flannels were smoldering. I jumped up and took off running for the river with half the camp following me. I didn't care. I jumped in the river and sat down almighty fast. I almost floated my hat!"

Kate began to giggle and said, "Go on."

"I got a new pair of red, flannel long underwear and tried them on. I was having trouble with them. I couldn't figure out why the buttons were down the back and the flap was in the front. Now, I was almighty bewildered. So, off I went to my campsite. I took them off and was standing there buck naked. A passel of Blackfoot squaws started laughing at me. My face turned red, and I tried to cover myself up."

Now she was laughing hard.

"I put it back on and still couldn't figure out why the buttons were in the back. I was downright uncomfortable standing there when some of my buddies wanted to play cards. The next thing I know, I'm sitting on an old blanket, holding a handful of greasy cards. My red flannels are on backward, and I'm barefoot. By now, everybody's laughing at me. Well, I started getting my dander up. Wasn't nobody going to make fun of me!"

"What did you do?" giggled Kate.

"I jumped up, threw my cards in the fire, and stomped off. The trapper who owned the cards got his mad going and came after me. He pulled his knife, and I pulled mine, and we went after each other. There I was, no moccasins on my feet, trying to hold my red flannels together with one hand and defend myself with the other."

"If that wasn't a sight!" laughed Kate.

"Kate, that ain't all! Trying to hold him off, I ripped the crotch out of my red flannels. Now, I'm half-naked again. He's trying to cut me, and it starts raining."

"Oh, no!" She laughed.

"I got away from him and went to my campsite. I sat down and pulled a blanket over my head. I was pulling my pants on when a herd of buffalo ran through the camp. That's when I woke up, looking for my rifle."

"Were you drunk?" she asked.

"No, Kate, I wasn't," answered Angus.

"Then what brought on this nightmare?"

"The only thing I can think of is that I ate it. We kept a stewpot going all the time. Every day, someone would toss something in the pot. The good Lord only knows what was in it."

Kate got a disturbed look on her face. "In your dream, you could have died!"

"I know it. I surely do. In my dream, I remember seeing a fresh skunk pelt hanging from a tree limb not far from the fire."

"You don't reckon?" she gasped.

"I don't know," said Angus. "It was just a dream."

"Sounds like a nightmare to me," mused Kate.

"I reckon it was," he answered.

"Why did you need your rifle?" asked Kate.

"To shoot the polecat who put the polecat in the stew pot!"

BLESSED

Angus couldn't sleep. He tossed and turned until Kate elbowed him in the ribs. Getting up, Angus dressed, went to the cookstove, and warmed a cup of leftover coffee. Going outside, he settled into his rocking chair.

"Lord, are you trying to tell me something?" Angus asked.

Immediately, a small voice spoke into Angus's spirit. "Go to the Trading Post."

Angus had heard the voice many times and knew who it was.

"Yes, Lord," he replied.

Making his way through the dark, Angus unlocked the Trading Post door and entered as quietly as possible. Rafe and Zeb were asleep in the back room, and he didn't want to wake them up.

Sitting in a chair by the cracker barrel, he softly said, "I'm here."

"Angus," said the voice. "Look around you. What do you see?"

"I see Trading Post supplies," answered Angus.

"I want you to be specific," said the Lord.

"I see all the leather goods that Aaron, Ava's husband, has made."

"What else do you see?" asked the Lord.

"I see Little Abner's woodwork. He's made a pile of tables and chairs. He has also repaired broken wagon wheels found along the trail."

"What else do you see?"

"I see a pile of Longhorn steer horns and hides my three eldest boys tanned for trade."

"And?"

"I see jars of honey from Alexander's beehives."

"And?"

"I see all the remedies and cures that Charles, Amelia's husband, has helped prepare for Rebeccah's apothecary shop."

"What else do you see?" asked the Lord.

"I see stacks of grain from Abraham's grist mill for sale or trade."

"Angus, what are these things?" asked the Lord. "Aren't they blessings?"

"Yes, Father, they are," Angus softly answered.

"Angus, I have blessed you ever since the day Jedediah Smith led you to me. Let me ask you something. Who caught the most beavers every year? I believe you did. Who kept you from being killed by the Arapahoes? Who watched over Kate and the children while you were gone?"

Angus didn't know what to say.

"Who led you to this valley and gave it to you? Who made sure Beaver Tail was here to intercede for you?"

"You did."

"Who got your parents here safely?"

"You did."

"Who watched over your boys when they went after the herd?"

"You did."

"Who put Katherine in your life? Who gave you eleven healthy children?"

"You did."

"Do you know why I did it?" asked the Lord.

"Is it because you love me?" asked Angus.

"Good answer, but there is more to it," said the Lord. "Angus, instead of a tithe of money, you gave of yourself. You were always there to help people and always told them about Me. Angus, you led many of them to me down through the years. I honored that because you honored me. You never thought twice about it. You just did it. Because of that, I am happy to bless you," said the Lord.

By this time, Angus was weeping softly before the Lord.

"Father," Angus sobbed, "I tried so hard to share Your Word. Some would listen, but most of them wouldn't. It breaks my heart to think about the ones that chose Hell."

"Angus, you couldn't save them all. Satan had too tight a grip on them."

"Father, I am so sorry," he sobbed.

"My child, you did your best," answered the Lord. "Now, look all around you at the blessings I have given you. Both of your clans are here, your quiver is full, and I am increasing your years."

"Father, thank You for Your love and blessings," Angus whispered.

"Well done, my good and faithful servant, well done."

A back door opened, and Rafe walked into the room.

"Angus? I thought I heard a voice. What brings you here at this hour?" asked Rafe.

"Just counting my blessings," smiled Angus. "Just counting my blessings."

THE BIRTHDAY

Angus would be the center of attention, and he hated it. Today was his birthday, and he wanted to forget it.

Kate had nudged him awake and kissed him. "Happy Birthday, you old coot!" she teased. What is it this year? Seventy-five?"

Angus looked at her and shook his head. "Kate, you know exactly how old I am."

"What's bothering you?" she asked.

"I'm getting old. I'm figuring I don't have much time left," Angus replied.

"Angus, are you feeling sorry for yourself?"

The look on his face told her the answer. Now she waited for him to tell her what was really going on.

"Kate, so many friends have gone under, and I'm still here. It doesn't rightly seem fair that I'm still alive. I watched them get killed by Indians, by critters, and by each other. Every time I celebrate another birthday, I can't help but think about them."

"Angus, it's normal to feel that way. You have to thank the good Lord you're still alive. Do you want to go under?" asked Kate.

"No, Kate, it isn't that. Birthdays just make me feel guilty, that's all."

THE BIRTHDAY

"I need you to do something for me," she said. "It's your seventy-fifth birthday. You know that all the family will be here. I want you to cheer up. If you don't, I'm going to whomp you good!"

Angus nodded and got out of bed. After breakfast, he saddled his horse and rode away.

Kate was sure she knew where Angus was going. The direction he took confirmed it.

"Lord, I ask that You help him," prayed Kate.

Angus reined in at Monument Rock and dismounted. He sat down on the bench that was in front of it. He let his eyes rest on the names and began to cry.

As Angus read the list of names, he spoke. "Hugh Glass, John Colter, I miss you sometimes fierce. When my birthday comes around, I think of you and how you were denied a long life."

As Angus spoke, he felt a presence around him. He turned in all directions to see if anyone was there. There was no one there. Puzzled, he closed his eyes and prayed.

"Father, is it you?" asked Angus.

A small voice spoke into his spirit, "Yes, Angus, it is I."

"Father," he said. "I hurt for my friends. Why am I still here?"

"Angus," the Lord answered. "You are here for your

family. I have allowed you a long life to ensure your family seeks and comes to Me."

"Father," he answered, "I have done my best to lead them to You."

"You have done well. Your family worships Me, and I am pleased. But Angus, you must let your friends go."

"But Lord, I can't."

"Angus, I will tell you something. All the witnessing you did for Me at the rendezvous was not in vain. You influenced many of your trapping friends. Some turned to me. Angus, you have trapping friends here with Me. They will greet you at the gate when your time has come."

Angus began to weep. Through his tears, he sobbed, "Thank You, Father, thank You."

"Now, your family is waiting for you. Go and enjoy your birthday."

Angus mounted up and rode to the church. All the family was there. Tables were on the lawn, and a steer roasted over hot coals. The women were setting the tables.

"Grandpa!" shouted the lads and lasses as he dismounted. His grandchildren immediately surrounded Angus. They took his hand and led him to the rocker at the head of the table.

When everything was ready, he got everyone's attention. He began to pray.

"Heavenly Father, I thank You for another year. But most of all, I thank You for my family," Angus said through tears.

While lying in Kate's arms that night, he told her what had happened.

"Kate, I have been selfish. All I could think about was my friends and what happened to them. I'm downright ashamed of myself," he softly spoke.

"Angus, I know that it's been hard on you. I'm glad the Lord spoke to you. Are you all right?"

"Yes, Kate. He told me something that made all the difference in the world. He told me my preaching was worthwhile. It eased my mind."

"You are a good man, Angus McDougal," she said while kissing him. "Happy Birthday."

"Thank you."

"Now, are you ready for your birthday present?"

"Kate?"

"Come here, you old coot!"

THE GLEN OF BLESSINGS

Angus lit his pipe and sat back in his rocker. It had been a long trip, and he was tired. The ranch house door opened, and Kate joined him. She scooted her rocker close to his, sat down, and held out her hand. Angus took hold and smiled at her.

"Thank you, you old coot!"

"For what?" he asked.

"Now, what do you think?"

He smiled, leaned over, and gave her a peck on the cheek. He knew what she was talking about. It was obvious. A little over a month ago, Kate had made a request. A request he was determined to fulfill.

She had brought it up while lying in bed.

"Angus, I'd like to see the glen before I go under. I've only seen a small part of it. Will you show it to me, please?"

The question had shocked him. And it disturbed him. He had been over every inch of the glen and knew it like the back of his hand. He realized he had been selfish. Kate had every right to see the beauty and grandeur of their home.

"We'll leave in a week. But first, we have to get ready."

A Conestoga wagon was taken from the cave, dismantled, and reassembled in Angus's barn for the trip. It was fixed with comfort in mind for Kate. Their sons had fastened their rockers to the wagon's side, and they put a mattress on the wagon's floor.

They had returned home the day before, worn out and happy. Now they were sitting on the front porch.

"What did you like the best?" asked Angus.

"Spending time with the lads and lasses," she answered with a smile.

"Kate, you see them every Sunday at church."

"I know. But the individual time spent was precious. In church, they have to behave. I wanted to see them being themselves. I wanted them to be comfortable around us. I think we accomplished it. The time spent with them is something they will remember for the rest of their lives," she answered.

"Aye, I agree. The wee ones climbed all over me as if I were a mountain. Having a pocket full of hard candy helped. I can still hear their laughter in my mind."

"Angus, they love you. They love both of us."

"Aye, I agree. This trip was a good thing. What else crosses your mind?"

"I can't get over how magnificent the glen is. Everywhere I looked, I saw God's handiwork. It is bonnie, that's for sure," answered Kate.

"Skeleton Canyon?"

Kate shuddered, rolled her eyes, and spoke. "I can't believe you took me there."

"It's part of the glen. You said you wanted to see everything," answered Angus.

"Not that place! It scares the daylights out of me. I'm sure enough glad you didn't take me in there. After what happened at the chicken coop, I'm surprised you would even consider going there!" She shuddered.

"Shadows Canyon?"

"Angus, I'm going to whomp you! I will admit seeing a little man with a shillelagh fascinates me. But you had no business taking me there!"

"Now, Kate!"

"Don't you 'now Kate' me. Remember what happened at the barn?"

Changing the subject, he spoke. "It was good seeing your family. It was wise to settle them at the Roaring Canyon entrance."

"It was bonnie. I had a good time with all the nephews and nieces. I miss my ma and pa something fierce. Anne, Cormac, James, and Ewan are doing well."

"Aye, your brothers and sister are happy there. Guarding that entrance is important. I'm glad they are there," said Angus. "Your brothers did a fine job building the gate across the entrance."

"Angus, I can't believe how many cattle we have. And the horses. The boys have outdone themselves," she gushed.

"Aye, Slim and the hands have taught the boys well. They have become regular cowhands," replied Angus. "Anything else?"

"Wheat Canyon and Abraham's grist mill. He has worked so hard. It's wonderful how everything turned out," she answered.

"Aye, he had a vision and made it happen. I'm proud of him."

"I almost forgot your family. I miss your ma and pa also."

"I miss them too. Pine Canyon entrance has been good for my brother and sisters. Guarding that entrance is vital. We all pitched in and built the gate across the opening. They seem to be happy there," said Angus.

"I saved the best for last," she said.

"What might that be?" asked Angus.

"The Trading Post. It has been wonderful. Especially since Atticus moved his blacksmith shop there."

"Aye, he gets a lot of business from people traveling the river," said Angus.

"Little Angus has his woodworking shop there. Rebeccah, Absalom's wife, has her apothecary shop; Aaron, Ava's husband, has his leather works; Charles, Amelia's husband, is the doctor and dentist. Jesse, Abigail's husband, doctors sick animals. Alexander has his beehives, and Abigail is the schoolteacher."

"Aye, it's a family venture. That's for sure. We have horses and cattle for sale and grain from the grist mill. We've done well for ourselves," said Angus.

"And we have something else," she offered with tears.

"And what might that be?" asked Angus.

"We have a preacher that loves his family."

Angus didn't know what to say.

"Do you realize how blessed we are?" she asked. "Just think about it."

Kate, you're right, of course. But we can't take the credit for it. It was God. None of this would have happened if He wasn't in our lives. We must never forget it."

Smiling, she spoke. "Pray, please!"

"Father, we thank You for Your blessings. You have been so good to us. I ask that You forgive us when we don't acknowledge You. It's not on purpose. We don't mean to ignore You. We get busy and forget. We ask that You continue to bless us. In Jesus's mighty name. Amen."

Kate squeezed his hand and agreed. "Amen."

THE STROKE

"Kate, I'm feeling poorly," muttered Angus.

"What seems to be ailing you," she said while putting down her rolling pin and coming to his side.

"My chest hurts, and my left arm feels funny. It's like someone is poking it with needles," Angus said in a garbled voice.

Trying to keep a happy face, Kate knelt by her husband, took his hand, and leaned in close so she could hear him.

Angus was breathing hard, and his face was an ashen gray color. Kate's grandpap had shown the same symptoms before he passed away. She remembered when old Doc Smuthers looked at him and shook his head.

"His ticker has gone bad," the old doc had said.

Kate remembered her granny asking if there was anything that he could do. She knew what the answer was by the look on the doctor's face.

"Just make him comfortable," she had been told. "There's nothing I can do. Sometimes they get over it. I'm not trying to build up your hope. It's in the Lord's hands now. If I were you, I'd start praying."

Kate remembered her granny and her siblings praying for her grandpap. They thought he was getting better until

THE STROKE

one afternoon he gasped, clutched his chest, and then was gone to meet his Maker.

Now Kate was facing the same thing with Angus.

"Angus," she asked, "how are you with the Lord?"

"Kate," he answered, "I reckon He and I are fine."

"We have to do a heap of praying. You have the same thing my grandpap had."

"What is it?" Angus asked.

"His heart went bad on him," answered Kate.

"Sounds serious," Angus said.

"It killed him," she softly spoke.

Angus got a concerned look on his face.

"Kate, I'm ready to meet the Lord. I truly am. But not today if I can keep from it."

"I'm not ready to give you up to Him yet. Not by a long shot!" Kate defiantly said.

Then Angus lapsed into unconsciousness.

Terrified, she went to the door, took a rifle down from the nearby rack, went out on the porch, and fired a round. In no time at all, she had family coming.

"Your Pa is ailing. Go to the church and ring the bell."

"How is he?" asked Alexander.

The look on her face told him it was serious.

"We are holding a prayer meeting at the church tonight. Spread the word!"

McDougal's Glen

The bell began to ring. The family and hired hands began showing up from the far reaches of the ranch. Except for the absolute essentials, ranch work came to a halt.

"Ma, what are we going to do without Pa?" cried Little Angus.

"Hush up!" she ordered. "He's not dead yet!"

Abigail volunteered to stay with Angus during the prayer meeting.

Kate went to the front of the church and spoke. "By now, all you know is Angus is poorly, and by what I've seen, I can tell it's his heart. He may survive, and he may not. In my heart, I know he won't if we don't pray. I need you more now than ever before." Then she knelt and began lifting her husband to the Lord.

The response was immediate. The entire family dropped to their knees and prayed.

After the meeting, Kate, flanked by her children, went home. Going to the door, they met Abigail.

"He's asleep. I can tell he's in pain. Is there anything we can give him?" She asked.

"Not that I know of. I'd give your pa a snort out of the jug, but I'm suspicious of it. It might do more harm than good."

"Ma," said Ansel, "you need some rest. I'll stay with him for a while."

THE STROKE

Kate nodded, sat down in her rocker, and dozed off.

Ansel woke her at midnight and said, "He seems to be doing better. His breathing is steady. He's not sweating like he was, and Pa has color coming back to his face."

"Praise the Lord," whispered Kate. "I'll stay with him now. You go home."

Sunlight was peeking through the window when she heard Angus's voice. Aggravated at having dozed off, she knelt by his side.

"Kate," he spoke in a garbled tone, "what happened?"

"Angus, I think you had what some people call a stroke. Something went wrong with your ticker. How do you feel?"

"I can't feel my left arm. It feels like a lump of wood," he answered.

"Can you lift it? Can you squeeze my hand?" Kate asked.

"I don't think so," Angus garbled. "What will I do?"

"You're going to lay there and go back to sleep! And that's an order!" replied Kate.

He looked at her and closed his eyes.

Someone knocked on the front door. It was Little Angus.

"Ma, how is Pa?"

"He's struggling. Go and ring the bell. We need to have

McDougal's Glen

another family meeting."

Kate stood in the front of the church and spoke. "Your pa is paralyzed on his left side and has garbled speech."

Cries of alarm filled the room.

"What can we do?"

"Make him as comfortable as possible and wait it out. He will need constant attention, so I need your help," confided Kate.

From that moment on, Angus had round-the-clock care. He was on everybody's prayer list and lifted to the Lord.

Angus's favorite place was the bench overlooking the glen. The boys would carry him up there, set him down in his rocker, and let him bask in the sun. They thought it would be good for him.

He sought the Lord daily. "Father, You know that I love You. You also know that I trust You. I know You will heal me because your Word says so. I have tried to live my life according to Your Word. Right now, in Jesus's name, I claim my healing. I give You praise for it. Amen."

He had to do it, and he made sure never to forget.

One afternoon, when he had finished praying, he felt in his spirit that something was about to happen. He lifted his face toward Heaven and said, "Father," and it happened. He felt a tingling in his left arm. As the tingling increased, his arm started getting hot. In his spirit, Angus heard a voice say, "Wiggle your fingers." Looking down, he watched as his fingers began to move. Then he heard the voice say, "Raise your arm." He lifted his arm toward Heaven and began praising God with an ungarbled voice.

When the door opened and Angus walked in, Kate was taking a pie out of the oven.

"Angus!" she cried as she dropped the pie on the floor.
She ran to him and took him into her arms.
"I don't understand," she cried.
"Kate, it was your prayers. It was everybody's prayers."
She began to tremble and had to sit down.
"The bell needs ringing," she cried.
"I'll do it," he said as he walked out the door.
And so he did.

McDougal's Glen

IT HAPPENED IN CHURCH

Angus pulled the rope with a heave, and the bell rang. He had taken it upon himself to ring the bell since they had settled the glen.

Angus had always been an early riser, and today was no exception. Years of living on the frontier had placed an invisible alarm clock into his brain. When the day broke, Angus was always up. His usual routine was stoking the fire and brewing a pot of coffee. Then, off to feed the livestock.

The only day Angus changed his routine was on Sunday. After feeding the livestock, he went home, changed clothes, and went to the church. There, he would build a fire, brew another pot of coffee, sit in his rocker, and pray for the service. Being the family patriarch and their preacher, Angus felt it was his responsibility to pray. As always, he prayed for the Lord to lead him. He depended on the Lord for leadership.

Now, he was calling his family and hired hands to worship. As the families arrived, Angus turned the bell ringing over to one of his grandsons. He then began greeting everyone as they came through the door.

IT HAPPENED IN CHURCH

As he greeted the family, Angus couldn't help but notice one of his newly hired hands was there. He didn't know much about him except that his name was Gus. Gus had ridden in one day asking for a job. The ranch always needed help, and he had hired Gus. Now, he was glad to see him in church.

When Angus saw that nobody else was coming, he went to the front of the church and began to pray. While doing so, he heard the Lord speak into his spirit.

"Angus, my child, I have something for you to do this morning."

Opening his eyes, Angus softly spoke. "Lord, I am here to do Your bidding."

"Ask Gus to come forth. I have something for him."

"Aye, Lord."

Looking toward the back of the room, he made eye contact with Gus. He immediately saw anxiety cross Gus's face. Gus got up and headed for the door.

"Gus," Angus said, "the Lord has told me He has something for you. Come to me, please, don't keep the Lord waiting."

Gus was afraid. You could see it on his face. He wasn't anticipating this when he walked through the church door. Now, he was the focus of everyone's attention.

"Preacher, why me?" he cried.

"Gus, I don't know. I'm doing what the Lord told me. Do you know the Lord? Can I pray with you?" asked Angus.

Gus came to Angus, stood before him, and spoke. "Yes, I know the Lord. I gave my heart to Him when I was a small boy. I love Him, I surely do."

Angus placed his hand on Gus's head and said, "Heavenly Father, send your power down on Gus."

The Holy Spirit arrived in all of His glory. No one could stand before Him. The power of His presence had put the entire congregation on the floor. Angus had taken hold of Gus's hand and could feel the Holy Spirit's power flowing from him.

Angus sat up and scooted beside him. He knew he had to wait on Gus.

Gus opened his eyes and looked at Angus. "What happened to me?"

"God happened," answered Angus with a smile.

"I knew when you started praying for me that something would happen. Something in my spirit told me so. The devil was telling me to run, and I almost did. I'm glad I didn't."

"Did God tell you to attend the service this morning?" asked Angus.

"Wild horses couldn't keep me away. I have known

for some time that I was supposed to come to McDougal's Glen. I kept hearing a voice telling me to come. I fought it for a while and then gave in. I know that I'm supposed to be here. I just don't know why," uttered Gus.

"God has something he wants you to do. He sent you here to do it," said Angus.

"I know it now, and what the Holy Spirit did proves it to me. I have never felt His power like that before. To be honest, I want to feel His presence again," he said.

"It isn't hard. All you have to do is to be humble and willing to let the Holy Spirit in. God knows when you are ready. The Holy Spirit will come if you want Him to," offered Angus.

"Will you help me?" asked Gus.

"Be glad to."

Angus and Gus began meeting once a week to study God's Word, pray, and seek Him. Gus didn't know how to read. Angus taught him how and gave him a Bible he had found among some abandoned goods along the trail. From that moment on, Gus had his nose stuck in it every chance he got.

One morning, Angus was praying when he heard the Lord speak.

"Angus, I am preparing Gus for the ministry. I have led him to you to be taught and to become your helper. When the time comes, he will replace you."

"Aye, Father, I understand. I will teach him what I know. Thank You for taking care of me and my family all these years. Thank You for allowing me to serve You."

"My child, you are approaching your time. I know you don't want to leave your family, and I understand it. I want you to know that you will see them in Heaven when their time is up. Not many people do I tell this. I tell you because you have been good and faithful to me. Be happy in this knowledge."

"Aye, Lord," answered Angus with tears in his eyes, "and thank You."

Angus told Kate what the Lord had said while lying in each other's arms.

Kate began crying, and Angus said, "Kate, don't cry. You should be thankful the Lord is raising someone to shepherd our family."

"You old coot!" she cried. "I'm not sad! I'm happy!"

"You make me proud that I married you," he whispered.

"I love you," Kate softly spoke.

"I love you," softly spoke Angus.

As he kissed her, he said, "Good night."

Kate rolled over and silently thanked the Lord for such a good man as Angus.

KATHERINE

Angus wept as he sat beside his wife. Kate had been feeling poorly, and neither he nor her family could figure out what was wrong. She had complained of chest pains and then collapsed. Angus knew that her family had a history of heart problems. It never dawned on him that her heart would give out on her.

Angus was holding Kate's hand while she was lying unconscious in their bed.

"Kate? Can you hear me?" he sobbed.

Not receiving a reply, he asked again, "Kate, can you hear me?"

He felt her hand move and took it that she had. Leaning close, Angus brushed her hair from her face and spoke.

"Kate, please don't leave me. I don't know what I will do without you," begged Angus.

From the front room came the sounds of the family. He had rung the bell, and everyone came as fast as they could. Each one had filed into the room to see their ma and was taken aback by what they saw. Not knowing what to say or do, the family silently waited for Angus to talk to them.

Angus went to his knees and began to pray for Kate.

"Father, I don't rightly know what is wrong with Kate. But You do. I am asking You to heal her in Jesus's mighty name."

When Angus finished, he began hearing the still, small voice he was so familiar with.

"Angus," said the Father, "I hear your prayers and see your anguish. What you ask, I am capable of doing. You know that I can. But Angus, I have allotted her so many years, and her time has come. Will you accept it?"

"Must I?" cried Angus. "Must I give her up? We have been together for almost seventy years."

"Angus, I have my reasons. You are seeing only a part of it. You are only seeing through your pain. You don't see the whole picture. You must trust Me. Can you do it?" asked the Father.

"Will I see her again?" Angus whispered through his tears.

"Kate will be waiting for you in the mansion you are to share. Your parents and hers will be there waiting for you and the five babies you lost," answered God.

Angus didn't know what to say.

"Angus, you need to look at it this way. It will be a happy reunion for all. After all, you will be in Heaven."

Resigned to the fact that Kate would be with the Lord, Angus spoke. "When will you take her home?"

"Tell your sons that you need them to help. Carry her in your arms as the boys move the bed out on the porch. I want all of the family to witness this," said God.

Angus called for his sons, and they did as God had instructed.

"Angus, take ahold of her hand," whispered God.

Hesitant and afraid, Angus did as God asked.

"Angus, can you hear the angels singing?"

Angus listened closely and began to hear the sounds of high-pitched voices.

"Yes, Lord, I can. Is it the angels?" asked Angus.

"Yes, my son, they accompany my children home."

Angus began to weep as he felt Kate's spirit leave her body.

"She is with me now," said the Lord. "She is home."

A CHISELED ROCK

The sun was warm on their backs as the McDougals slowly ascended the knoll to the family cemetery. On their shoulders, the sons of Angus McDougal bore his casket. In the distance, the church bell was ringing, its peals adding to the solemnness of the occasion.

Mourners had come from miles around to honor the passing of the patriarch of the proud family. Even a handful of his trapping buddies had made the trip.

The sons had dug a grave beside Kate's resting place atop the knoll. They had chiseled a slab of rock with both of their names when their mother had passed. They had buried their grandparents on both sides of the site, with Kate's beside her and Angus's beside him.

The procession was long and silent. Over the years, the family had grown by leaps and bounds. Grandchildren and great-grandchildren walked by their parents, each carrying a handful of wildflowers to lay across the gravesite.

As they gathered near, Ansel took the family Bible and read the twenty-third psalm. It was their father's favorite, and he had quoted it many times. When finished, Ansel asked, "How many remember him quoting those verses?"

Hands shot up everywhere until everyone's hands were up.

McDougal's Glen

"I know that Pa walked through the valley of the shadow of death many times. The Lord was with him each time. Now, he is walking hand in hand with Ma in Heaven. The valley they are walking through has no dangers or evils. Now they are in our Heavenly Father's hands, and I am proud to know it.

"As we put him beside Ma, we must say goodbye to a legend. Our pa was known far and wide for his honesty, courage, and generosity. That is how we should always remember him. I know I will.

"We plan to keep his tradition going. He loved his family and would want us to stay together. Being his children, we are determined to do so. And by God, we will," Ansel said as he closed the Bible.

As his sons lowered him into his grave, tears fell like rain. As the family passed by, they gently tossed handfuls of dirt on his coffin, and the grandchildren placed their flowers.

As the mourners slowly descended the knoll, a handful separated from them and went in a different direction.

Stopping at Monument Rock, the old trappers chiseled his name.

Printed in the USA
CPSIA information can be obtained
at www.ICGtesting.com
CBHW070731100124
3328CB00004B/110

9 798890 417060